To Melissa

Tease

KINGS OF KORRUPTION
novel

Happy reading!

by

GERI GLENN

Geri Glenn

Tease is a work of fiction. Names, characters, places, and incidents are the products of the author's imagination and are used fictitiously. Any resemblance to actual events, locales, or persons, living or dead, is entirely coincidental.

Cover Art
Wicked by Design

Editing
Ready, Set, Edit

Formatting
Tracey Jane Jackson
www.traceyjanejackson.com

2015 Geri Glenn
Copyright © 2015 by Geri Glenn
All rights reserved.

ISBN-10: 151930160X
ISBN-13: 978-1519301604
Published in the United States

I don't even know where to start! So many people had a hand in helping me with this project and I never could have done it without them.

To My Hubby – Mike, I know that living with a crazy writer (well me anyways) is not always fun, and there have been so many times that you've wanted to run screaming. Thank you for sticking it out and doing more than your share around this house while I focus on my dream. You are a wonderful husband and the girls are lucky to have you as their dad to take good care of them and show them what a good man is really like. I may not say it enough, but I love you!

To Amanda DiPierro– For someone just starting out as a PA, you have kicked ass girl. I ask a whole lot of you and you always go above and beyond. I'm thankful for all that you do and am looking forward to continuing this journey with you by my side. Love ya lady.

To Christina DeRoche – Again, you read every section of my work as I write it and always deliver honest and extremely valuable advice. Your opinion means the world to me, and these books have almost as much of you in them as they do me! I could never have gotten Tease right without you. P.S. You are never allowed to leave the country to go to tropical climates when I am on a deadline ever again!

To Jacqueline Sinclair – Once again, you're professional opinion and advice has been invaluable. I enjoy our late night rants, giggles and words of encouragement. Meeting you has been one of the most rewarding parts of this self-publishing journey and I can't wait until we actually meet in person.

To Shelly Morgan – You have been amazing though all of this. Not only have you pointed me in the direction of amazing cover designers and editors, you also took the time out of your very busy schedule to make me some beautiful and very sexy teasers! You are one talented lady, and I am excited to meet you for real in Mississippi!

To Robin From Wicked By Design – Yet again, you've created me a gorgeous cover that I am proud to show off and that people love to stare at. Your work is incredible and you are always so helpful when I need extras. You have developed a fan for life, girl!

To Shannon From Shanoff Formats – Thank you! You saved my ass at the last minute with Ryker and you have been amazing with Tease. I don't remember how I found you, but I thank God that I did!

To My Queens – You girls have been so amazing. I can't tell you how many times you ladies have made me smile when I go to post a promo pic or do a takeover and see that you ladies are way ahead of me. Your loyalty is humbling and your friendship is so very valued. I look forward to meeting every one of you someday, and maybe get a real life pic that doesn't involve Johnna in a sink.

To The Bloggers – So many bloggers have supported me along the way, I would need a whole other book just to list them. I try to thank you all as you post, and your reviews and support have been incredible. I am so thankful for all that you do. Without awesome bloggers like you, lowly indies like me wouldn't have a chance in hell.

To Avelyn Paige and her Saints & Sinners – Thank you for helping me put together such a huge release blitz. It hasn't happened yet, but so many people are on board and that is all because of you. I appreciate all the help you give me and if I can ever return the favor, I am at your service!

To Maria Lazarou – Not only did you design me some amazing book trailers, you also helped out with a ton of promotion for both Tease and Hybrids. I don't know where you find the time to do all that you do, but know that I appreciate it so much and will be recommending you far and wide!

To My Readers – I am also thankful for all of you. I am thankful that you have taken a chance on a little Canadian girl who loves books and I hope that I didn't disappoint you. For every email, follow, review and purchase, from the bottom of my heart, thank you.

I dedicate this book to my mom, a woman who has shown me what it takes to be a strong, independent woman and has never given up on me. We've had our share of trials and every time, you've been there with unconditional love and support. I am who I am because of you. Thank you for making me the type of person who has the courage to reach for the stars. I love you Mom.

Laynie

"**N**O, BUDDY! SHHH! I pull the little terrier closer, trying to calm and quiet him. If Rick hears him barking again, he'll kill him. He'd said so himself. Rick is my new stepfather, and he is mean. He smells bad too. I'll never understand why my mother had to go and marry that big jerk in the first place.

I miss my real dad. He was the best dad ever – but then, last year when I was only eight years old, he died. My mom blames me; I know she does, even though she says that's not true. The fire chief said it was an electrical fire. I'd been sound asleep when the smoke detectors went off. The air in my room had been thick with black smoke, choking me and making it hard to breathe. I tried so hard to get out of my room, but the door handle was just too hot. I tried to open the window too, but I just wasn't strong enough to lift it. I was trapped.

I was so scared. Buddy was scared too. He crawled right under my bed and curled up into a little ball, shaking with fear. I was screaming and crying, trying with all my might to yank open the window. I even tried to break it, but I just wasn't strong enough. After giving up on the window, I crawled under that bed with Buddy and hugged him close. Squeezing my eyes closed, I prayed for someone to rescue me.

That's when I heard a loud crash as my Dad broke the window from the outside. He was standing on a ladder, like my very own superhero, hollering for me to come on. I couldn't get Buddy, though. He had pushed back even farther under the bed, too terrified to come out. I crawled farther under, ignoring my father's panicked order to hurry. Flames were now coming through the walls, and I was choking on the filthy air, coughing and gagging.

Just as I got my hand on Buddy's collar, someone grabbed my ankle, hauling me out from under the bed. My dad had come into the room. I cradled Buddy to my chest as he turned me, hurrying toward the window. He tucked Buddy into my shirt and lifted me up and over the window ledge. After waiting for me to get my feet situated, he'd looked me right in the eye and told me not to look down.

I'd made it down about six rungs when the ceiling fell in. My Dad never made it out of that room.

Now Mom was married to Rick; she met him at some bar a few months ago, and within just a couple of weeks, we'd moved into his house far away from any of my friends. Dad would have hated him. He drinks too much, and now so does my Mom. She barely talks to me at all anymore. She says I look too much like my dad, and it hurts to even look at me. Buddy and I keep to ourselves most of the time, but when they start fighting — which they do a lot — Buddy barks.

They're fighting right now which is why Buddy won't shut up. He doesn't like it when Rick calls my mom nasty names any more than I do – I hate that he talks to her like that – I hate *him*. Wrapping my hand around Buddy's snout, I shush him once more. His small body trembles with anxiety.

Just then, the door slams open, bouncing off the wall. "Give me that fuckin' dog!" he roars. Rick stands in the doorway, a large butcher knife clutched in his fist. Jumping to my feet, I block Buddy's body with my own.

"I told ya what would happen if you didn't keep that fuckin' thing quiet. Give him to me!"

"No!" I scream. "You can't have him! He's mine."

Rick surges into the room just as Mom comes around the corner, tears gleaming on her cheeks. I pick Buddy up, turning him away from Rick and look frantically for a way to get out of the room. I'm not fast enough. Rick swings out, his fist connecting with my cheek and knocking me back onto the floor.

Buddy leaps from my arms, teeth bared as he growls and snaps at Rick. Mom is screaming something, but my head is still ringing from the punch he'd just given me. Just as I am able to stand, Rick gets his hand around Buddy's neck and lifts him high in the air.

Buddy's feet scramble to push against his forearm, eyes bugging out of his head. Rick raises the knife to Buddy's throat, ready to slash across it, stealing the only family I have left since my dad died.

"Let him go!" I run, slamming into him from the side, knocking him off balance and causing him to drop the tiny dog. Rick's long arm darts out, grabbing me by the collar of my shirt before he yanks me back. He throws me to the floor and climbs on top of me, pinning me down with his large body.

The air is filled with my screams, my mom's cries, and the constant barking of my best friend. Rick's hand flies out, slapping me across the side of my head with all his might. I stop screaming, my head swimming. I can see Mom pulling at his arm, trying to lift him off of me. He swings back that arm, knocking her to the floor as well. She doesn't move when she lands.

Turning back to me, Rick lifts his knife to my face. "You little shit! I should fuckin' kill you for that." He doesn't even see Buddy coming. Buddy rushes him from the side, latching onto his arm, biting and shaking like a full-grown Rottweiler.

With his free hand, Rick reaches around and grabs the little dog by the head once more. Lifting him by the throat, he whips his arm viciously back and forth. I hear a small yelp before Buddy drops to the floor, his tongue hanging limply from his mouth.

An anguished cry escapes my throat as I stare at my beloved Buddy. He's dead – I know it. His lifeless eyes are staring at me as Rick turns back to me, sneering in my face as he raises his knife. He places the tip of it right under my eye, the cold steel pressing deep enough to draw blood.

"I'm gonna teach you not to fuck with me. EVER!" Pressing his blade in farther, he draws it from my eye, down my cheek, and stopping at my chin. The pain is excruciating as he slices my skin. I scream in pain and humiliation. "Next time, I'll fuckin' kill you!"

He grabs my shoulders and lifts me slightly off the floor before slamming me back down again, my head cracking off the hardwood.

Standing, he curls his lip at me. "Piece of shit." He walks out of the room then, leaving me with my dead dog, my unconscious mother, and my mangled face.

Laynie

I PLACE MY hand on the door handle and push it open just as someone from the other side yanks it toward. With my hand still on the handle, I stumble forward, hurriedly putting my hands out in front of me to prevent smashing my face off the sidewalk. I don't make it that far, though. My hands connect with a wall of solid muscle.

"Sorry." The word is muttered from a gruff and smoky voice coming from about a foot above my head. I'm five foot eight so that means this guy must be very tall. By habit, I tilt my face toward his and smile.

"No worries." I move my fingers slightly and hear his swift intake of breath. That's when I realize that my hands are resting on his *very* firm torso. I can feel the rough outline of his abs through his shirt. I want nothing more than to explore further, and maybe even count them, but chances are, that might be creepy. Standing upright, I readjust my hold on Dexter's harness and pull away slightly, inhaling his scent as I go. He smells like worn leather and motor oil mixed with a hint of cologne. That smell is the sexiest thing ever to pass through my nostrils.

Realizing that I'm just standing there awkwardly smelling the poor man, I give him a tight smile and gently tug on Dexter's lead, letting him know that it's time to go. I feel him step aside, and my shoulder brushes his chest as I pass. I inhale his scent one last time before stepping out into the cool autumn afternoon.

Grinning like a fool, I make my way down the busy street, heading toward home. I'm not one bit embarrassed that I just felt up that delicious-smelling man. I don't often get the opportunity to lay my fingers on such fine, toned flesh – like, ever.

Moving down the sidewalk, I put ab man out of my mind and think back to this morning and my counseling session with Max. Max is an eleven-year-old boy who has lost most of his vision over the course of the last year. My job, as his Vision Loss Counsellor, is to help him accept his blindness as his new reality and find something for him to be excited about again.

Today had gone well, and I'd finally noticed some progress. Max even learned to play a chord on the guitar. Over the past couple of months, I had tried to help him find something – anything – to be excited about, but Max is just pissed at the world. He's pissed he can't play video games with his friends anymore. Pissed that he can't go outside and play road hockey with the neighborhood kids like he used to. Mostly, Max is pissed because he loves sports, mostly soccer, and he just can't play that anymore. In his young mind, his life is over.

Last week I had given him one of the loaner guitars and an instructional CD for children that the hospital loaned out to patients of their various programs. He had taken it, but I could hear the doubt coloring his voice; he was just too polite to voice it. But the fact that he had gone home, listened to that CD and taught himself a chord on the guitar – I call that progress.

I love my job. The hours are flexible, and I get to mentor some amazing kids in an area that I am passionate about. My blindness happened when I was seventeen. At first, I had been devastated, but then I realized that being blind is only a small part of who I am. It doesn't have to define me. I was a strong and independent girl before it happened, and now I am an even stronger, more independent woman. To be able to help children realize the same thing for themselves is an amazing feeling.

I know we've reached my building when Dexter slows, angling his body slightly to press against my leg. This is my cue to slow down. As we slow to a stop, I raise my hand, searching for the keyhole to the main door of the old stone house that holds four separate apartments, one of which I rent for an insane amount of money. The apartment itself is huge, and its location is perfect, allowing me to walk just about everywhere I need to go, but I pay for it.

Dexter leads me up the familiar staircase to the doorway of my unit. Once inside, I lock the door before turning and giving him an affectionate scratch behind the ear. I unhook his harness, relieving him of his working duty. As a Guide Dog, Dexter is trained to be in work mode from the minute that harness goes on in the morning until I take it off in the evening. During that time, he is focused entirely on his job and ensuring my safety. Once it comes off, though, he is just like any other gigantic lap dog.

He runs off in search of his stuffed rabbit while I move toward the kitchen to start making supper. On the way, I stop to check for messages on my answering machine. Within thirty seconds of it playing, I wish I had left that task until later.

As I walk down the hall, my mother's nasally voice fills the apartment around me.

"Laynie, it's your mother. I didn't get a chance to talk to you yesterday, and I'm worried. You know I like to talk to you every night." I roll my eyes, waiting for it to end, but she keeps talking. "You need to call me, young lady. I need to know that you're OK. I need to hear your voice, honey. Please call me back."

Entering the kitchen, I go straight to the fridge and pull out the lasagna that was left over from the night before while the next message plays. My mother again.

"Laynie Marie! I'm now officially worried. Call me back immediately!"

God! My mother drives me up the wall. I love her to pieces, but she is a shameless worrywart that hovers around me at all times.

Even from three hours away, she still manages to keep tabs on me. I can't escape her.

The next message is from my brother, Daniel. "Laynie? Mom's freakin' out. Why do you do this to her? You need to call her. She wants me to pop over and check on you. Call me."

Yanking my lasagna from the microwave, I make my way over to the couch and dig in to my supper. Filled with frustration, I think about my family, wondering when they are going to realize that I'm a grown ass woman, and I need to live my own life. If I had my sight, would they still treat me this way? They may still have *their* sight, but they don't really *see* me for who I really am; I'm not sure if they ever will…if *anyone* ever will.

Tease

It had never been my intention to talk to her. I'd only come into the coffee shop to get a closer look. I wish now that I hadn't. She was even hotter up close, and fuck me, she smelled like goddamned strawberries. A whole fucking field of them. It made me want to taste her.

I'd first seen her a couple weeks ago when I'd been keeping tabs on Charlotte, my buddy Ryker's woman. Charlotte works at a nursing home directly across the street from The Bean, a hipster-type coffee shop that I normally wouldn't be caught dead in. I drink my coffee black. Coffee isn't meant to have fucking whipped cream and chocolate shit drizzled all over it.

But today, I did go in. I went in because I couldn't fucking take it anymore. Every time Charlotte worked, I sat outside, watching the shop for another glimpse of this woman, and every fucking time, there she was. I needed to see her close up. To see if her hair was as golden as it seemed to be from across the street. I needed to see what color her eyes were and whether her figure was as smoking as it was from a distance. It was. Fuck, all of it was. I never did see what color her eyes were, though. They'd been hidden by a large pair of round framed sunglasses.

When I pulled that door open, I had no clue she was on the other side. She comes flying at me, landing against my chest, her strawberry scent filling my nostrils. A muttered apology is all I can manage. I don't know what the fuck to say. She is there, right in front of me – fucking touching me — and I freeze. I don't want to scare her, which is odd because I *like* being scary. I've worked at it.

I just stand there like a complete fucktard and stare at her. It all happens so fast; I'm still frozen when she smiles tightly at me and walks away. Stepping out of the shop behind her, I watch as she struts down the street, her ass swaying seductively in her long, tight-fitting dress.

After she turns the corner, her Guide Dog leading the way, I shake my head and go back to my post outside the nursing home. Now that I've seen her up close, I have more questions than before. What is her name? Why is she at the coffee shop each day, always at the same time? What color *are* her eyes?

I'm curious about her Guide Dog. Is she blind? She doesn't seem to be, but she always has those glasses on, and her dog is always with her. He wears a Guide Dog harness and vest, and it says Canadian Deaf Blind Association right on it. And why the fuck does she smell like strawberries?

I don't know why I care. It's not like I will ever find out. It's not like I want to. There's no room in my heart for her. I'm pretty sure my heart's dead anyways – black and shriveled. It died a long time ago, back when I was just a kid. I've been broken for as long as I can remember, and nothing will ever fix the fucked up pieces of my soul. The truth is, I don't even want to. Everybody that I have ever loved has contributed to the fucked up mess that is my life, and I never want to love another person ever again.

A bitch like that would be scared shitless of a mean son-of-a-bitch like me anyways – as she should be.

Tease

I'VE BECOME A fucking stalker. A creepy, over-caffeinated stalker. For the last couple of months, ever since the day we collided, I've gone to that hippie coffee shop, ordered a black coffee and sat on the patio, one table away from her. In those months, my whole world has gone to hell. I'd been working with a young as fuck, new prospect, Ryker's woman had been kidnapped and almost killed, causing a whole shit storm with another club. The stress of it all would have been almost unbearable if it weren't for my mystery woman. Sounds creepy as hell, but being near her calms me somehow. I still don't even know her name, and I haven't dared to speak to her, but at least three times a week I've sat close by. While watching her, I've learned plenty.

I've learned that she is definitely blind, but that doesn't seem to hold her back any. She moves with confidence and grace, only relying on the dog when necessary. I've learned that she's a writer, or a blogger or some shit. She's always on her laptop, earphones in her ears, fingers wildly plucking away at the keyboard. I've learned that when she's thinking, she twirls her hair. Often, her fingers on the keyboard stop their race across the keys, her head tilts slightly to the side, and she pulls a chunk of her honey blonde hair between her fingers and twirls. This can go on for quite a while and every time she does it, I can't help but wonder what the fuck she's thinking about.

My favorite thing I've learned about her is that when she's concentrating, her little pink tongue pokes out the side of her mouth just a tiny bit. It makes me hard every single time.

I don't know why I keep coming back here, torturing myself with what I can never have, or why I am doing this creepy stalker shit. The only thing I can say is, she's got my attention, and I can't get her out of my fucking head.

As she types and drinks her chocolate drizzled, girly coffee, her German Shepard lies silently under the table, head always up and alert, watching his surroundings. I can smell her strawberries from where I'm sitting, and it still continues to fuck with my head.

Like every other day, at six o'clock on the dot, an alarm sounds on her phone. She packs up her computer and earbuds, stuffing them into a hideous, neon pink backpack. I love this part of my stalking best because this is when I get to hear her voice.

"Come on, Dex." Her voice sounds like sex – husky and sensual. If she sounds like this when she's just talking to her dog, I can't help but wonder what she'd sound like if I got my mouth between those creamy white thighs of hers.

Slowly, she stands, swinging her bag over one shoulder, hand clasping the handle of the dog's harness. I watch as he slowly leads her away from the chair, around her table, and past my own. Just as she passes, mere inches from where I sit, she pauses. Her head tilts down in my direction, and I swear at that moment that she's looking right at me.

I freeze, staring up at her, wondering if I've been busted. My dead heart pounds erratically in my chest as we stare at one another for what feels like several minutes. She leans forward slightly, and if I'm not mistaken, takes a deep sniff. *Did she just fucking smell me?*

My face heats, and I sit up straight, unsure of what to do. And then she smiles. I can't breathe. She's smiling directly at me, her entire face lighting up with pure delight. She has the wonkiest, most fucked up smile I've ever seen. It's beautiful. *She's* beautiful.

"Hi again." She keeps grinning at me as she speaks, and it takes me a minute to realize that she's talking to me. *Shit! Can she see me?*

"Uh...hey." *Real smooth, asshole.*

Her smile widens with amusement. "Maybe tomorrow, instead of sitting all the way over here, you can join me at my table."

I stare at her in shocked silence as she stares back from behind those dark sunglasses, waiting for my response. Anger courses through me like wildfire. *She* can *fucking see me. She's seen me all along.* This bitch is playing with me, and I don't like it.

I curl my lip, sneering at her. "Not fuckin' likely."

Her smile falls a fraction, disappointment flashing across her face before she straightens, clears her expression of all emotion, and shrugs. "All right. Your loss."

I don't say a word as she turns, gives the harness a gentle tug, and steps out of the fenced area of the patio onto the busy sidewalk. My mind is spinning. I thought she was fucking blind. All this time she knew I was watching her, and she likely thought I was a fucking pervert or some shit. She'd been making fun of me when she'd invited me to her table. That's the way passive aggressive bitches like her work.

As she leaves, passing in front of the patio with her head held high, I hear a commotion from farther down the sidewalk. Swinging my head in that direction, I see people crying out as they jump out of the way of a bicycle careening down the sidewalk at top speed.

Whipping my head back to her, I see her turn, stepping farther out into the middle of the sidewalk as she tries to figure out what the commotion is. That's when I realize, she really *can't* see. She is looking in the direction of the noise, but there is no way in hell she can see that she's about to be run over by that bike. If she did, she wouldn't be just standing there.

I jump up from my seat, moving to vault over the waist-high fence of the patio as I holler out a warning. "Look out!"

The bike is just about to her. The kid on it has a purse clutched in one hand, his entire torso turned, looking behind him and not in the direction that he's going. He's going to hit her – there's no way I will make it to her in time.

Just then, her dog angles his body in front of hers, using his weight to push her back against the patio fencing. My feet clear the fence, and I land beside her just as the dog lets out an ear-piercing yelp.

Laynie

It all happened so fast. The worst part is, I don't even know what the hell it was that happened at all. I was walking away, trying not to show my humiliation at the way that my regular coffee neighbor had shot me down when I had heard a bunch of yelling and movement behind me. I'd turned to look just as I heard Coffee Dick yell out a warning. Next thing I know, my own dog had shoved me against a fence.

I'd heard a crash of metal, several thuds, and then Dexter had let out a long, ear-piercing scream of pain. Coffee Dick came out of nowhere. Now I'm knelt down, hands out, frantically patting the air around me as I tried to find Dexter.

"He's right here." His hand grasps my own and moves it down and to the left until it rests on Dexter's head. "He's hurt."

Just then, a groan comes from a few feet away. Coffee Dick growls, and I can feel his pissed off energy pouring off of him. "You stupid fuck. What the fuck were you thinkin'?" His voice has moved, and I know instantly that he's moving toward whatever "stupid fuck" he's talking to.

I can hear a crowd of rubberneckers gathering around us as I pat along Dexter's body, looking for any sign of bumps or bleeding. Coffee Dick is knelt beside me again, muttering to himself something about body bags and deep holes. Suddenly he's standing, and he's taking my dog with him.

Grasping my hand in his own, he places it on his hip. Surprised and confused, I yank it away. "Babe. We gotta move. Hook onto my belt loop."

"What?" *What's going on?*

"Your dog is hurt. We need to get him to a vet. To do that, we gotta move. Now hold onto my fuckin' belt."

In no position to argue, I reach back down, locate his belt loop, and hook my pointer finger through it. He starts moving, and I have to jog to keep up with him. "He's really hurt?"

"Yeah. May have a broken leg. He's holdin' it funny." I tuck my body close to his and hold on tight as he weaves his way through pedestrians. "Call a taxi. Have them meet us at the corner of Bleeker and St. James."

"A taxi?"

He doesn't answer. He just keeps moving, dragging me along behind him. I pull out my phone, asking Siri to dial the number for the taxi service I always use. I place the call, requesting the pick up where Coffee Dick had said, while he pulls to a stop. Raising my hand, I locate Dex and gently stroke his head which is resting on Coffee Dick's bicep.

I realize then that his name very likely isn't Coffee Dick, and he *is* doing me a favor so, even though I am pretty sure he's an asshole, maybe I should find out his actual name. "I'm Laynie."

I continue to stroke Dexter's head, my hand accidentally-on-purpose brushing along his bicep. It's huge and hard as a rock. I feel him tense when I speak; he doesn't answer me, though.

"You have a name?"

"A name?" He sounds uncomfortable.

"Yeah. You know…a name. Something I can call you besides Coffee Dick?"

He lets out a surprised snort. "Coffee Dick? Why the fuck would you call me Coffee Dick?"

"Because you're always at the coffee shop…and you're kind of a dick. Coffee Dick."

Amusement laces his voice as he turns to face me. "Tease. Call me Tease. Just don't fuckin' call me Coffee Dick. Ever."

"Tease?" I wrinkle my nose in confusion. "What kind of mother names her kid Tease?"

"It's not the name my mother named me. It's the name I go by."

Why somebody would ever choose to go by the name Tease is beyond me, but I can tell this is important to him...so I push anyway. "Well, I like Coffee Dick better than Tease."

Silence surrounds me for a moment before I hear the sound of a car pulling up beside us. Taking my hand in his, *Tease* moves forward, placing my hand on the top of the door, allowing me to feel my way inside the vehicle. I scooch my bootie over to the far side and he lowers himself in beside me with Dexter on his lap. I tell the driver which veterinarian's to take us to and we're off.

Again, I reach over, placing my hand on Dexter's head, stroking his ears the way he loves it. The cab is silent, and my thoughts start running wild. Worry for my dog moves to the forefront of my mind. I don't know what I will do if the poor bugger's leg is broken. Part of me wants to go back and kill that careless kid for hurting him.

"Travis."

His voice pulls me from my worries, bringing me back to the present where I am crammed into the back of this tiny cab with a complete stranger and my wounded dog. "Uh...sorry. What?"

"Travis. My mother named me Travis." His voice is soft and spoken almost directly into my ear. I feel like he just let me in on an enormous secret. Goosebumps race across my skin.

I turn slightly to face him. "Now *that* I like. Travis is way better than Coffee Dick." I smirk a little and am rewarded with a slight chuckle.

The taxi pulls to a stop, the driver calling out the total for our fare. I reach for my purse but hear the driver thank us and Travis is getting out of the car. Scrambling out on my side, I place my hand on the trunk, using it to guide my way to the sidewalk. Travis nabs my hand, once again placing it on his waist. I fumble for his belt loop as I say, "I would have gotten that."

"Don't worry about it." We enter the vet's office, and Travis takes us straight to the desk. After a quick explanation of what happened, the receptionist moves us right to an exam room. I hear Travis set Dex down on the table, and then he grabs my hand, pulling me up to the edge.

The natural way that he guides me without thought makes my

head spin. Even my family is awkward and obvious when assisting me with any task. I hate that. It makes me feel like an invalid and completely useless. Depending on people is not my strong suit, and I don't do it unless I absolutely have to.

Just then, his phone rings. "I gotta take this. Be right back."

He leaves the room, leaving me alone with Dexter. I bend at the waist, lowering myself so that I can rub my cheek along the top of his head. "My poor boy. We're gonna get you fixed up, OK?"

A warm, wet, doggie kiss is planted on my cheek, and I smile. It's sad to admit, but Dexter is the best friend I've ever had. He's insanely smart, never judges me – regardless of the fact that he's seen me naked – and he is always happy to see me. Even before I lost my vision, I'd never had a true, loyal friend. Dexter is one of the best things to ever happen to me.

The door opens, and I hear the footsteps of someone entering the room. Lifting my head, I turn toward the noise.

"I hate to do this to ya, but I've gotta go. It's an emergency."

I nod my head and smile, worried for him and hoping that it's nothing too terrible. "OK. I hope everything is all right."

"Yeah. It's just…work shit. Ya know?"

I nod again in understanding. "I do. Well, hey…thanks for your help with Dex."

"Didn't do much." He clears his throat. "But you're welcome." An awkward silence fills the room. "Well…see ya later, Laynie. I hope your dog's OK."

Just as his footsteps fade from the room, I turn, dashing toward the door. "Travis! Wait —" My foot catches on the edge of something – a chair leg, I think – and I stumble, throwing my hands out in front of me to catch myself.

My knees crack off the ceramic tile flooring, my hands landing with a loud slap. His return footsteps pound across the floor as he runs to help me. "Shit! Laynie? Are you OK?"

Feeling like an ass, I nod and struggle to get to my feet. Travis doesn't help me, and I like that. Somehow he knows that his help would only make it even more humiliating for me. "I'm fine." I fake a smile, wondering if my face is as red as it feels. "Happens all the time."

Reaching out, I feel my way back to the examination table, skimming my fingers through Dexter's fur and searching for my wounded pride. He clears his throat, reminding me that he was in a hurry to leave. "I just...well..." *Why the hell am I nervous now? Jeez, Laynie, get a grip!* "Can I, uh...get your number? So I can pay you back for the taxi?"

Clearly offended, he growls, "I can afford a fuckin' taxi, Laynie."

Shit. I didn't mean to offend him. "I know. I just...I just wanted to pay you back, OK? It's important to me." I face him head on, hoping that he doesn't argue with me on this. I hate to owe things to people. I'm not a charity case.

He groans. "Fuck. Whatever. Give me your phone."

Biting back my smile of victory, I hand over my phone. I hear the clicking of the touchscreen buttons before he hands it back to me. "There. Happy?"

I can't help my grin now. Beaming at him, I give him an exaggerated nod.

He chuckles. "Fuckin' nut." I hear him come closer and the jingle of Dexter's collar from where Travis is petting him. "Be cool, Dex. Later, Laynie."

My belly is overrun with a swarm of warm butterflies. "Later."

Tease

AFTER THE CAB delivers me to my bike, I swing my leg over and peel out of the parking lot, still trying to work out in my head what the fuck just happened. After months of watching her, I'd finally spoken to her and found out her name. *Fucking Laynie.* How I went from silently watching her from behind my coffee cup to having her smile up at me with amusement blows my fucking mind. She'd teased me – like flat out fucking teased me – and for the first time in years, I didn't lose my shit. Instead, I wanted nothing more than to crush my mouth to hers, wiping that goofy smile off her flawless face.

I don't kiss, though. I've never kissed. I don't caress or cuddle or do pillow talk. My relations with women consist of grabbing a club whore, bending her over, doing what I need to do to get off and then zipping up my pants. End of story. If she gets off, good for her – I don't give a shit either way.

Ever since the night I got my hideous scar, I've known that I was ugly. Women take one look at me and run. I like it that way – I'm used to it. Maybe that's why it was easier to talk to Laynie, though, to actually have a conversation with a woman. She couldn't see me, didn't know the monster she thought had saved her. If she could, she would never have taunted me. Hell, she'd never even have spoken to me in the first place.

But she did. And she'd made me smile. I don't even remember the last time I'd smiled. What the fuck is there to smile about? The woman is clearly crazy.

Pulling up to the clubhouse, I see a ton of bikes parked in a row and cars parked in every available spot. The music is thumping, and the sounds of laughter and conversation fill my ears. This isn't unusual for a Saturday night around here. Things can get pretty wild.

Usually, I don't mind coming to these parties, but I've been fucking busy. For the first time since I became a prospect, I had something of my own to do and these fuckers had called me away. I had no choice, though. As a prospect, the brothers of the Kings of Korruption can feed me all the shit they want, and I have to eat it without complaint. Staying at the vet's with Laynie would be a waste of time, anyway. A bitch like that and a monster like me don't even belong in the same city, let alone the same conversation.

When I walk inside, the music and laughter stop completely. *What the fuck?* I stand in the doorway, looking around the room and see the eyes of every single person in it are focused on me. My skin crawls and my insecurities quickly turn to a slow-burning anger. I fucking hate it when people stare at me. The scar on my face never fails to draw the attention that I avoid at all costs.

Just then, Ryker steps forward from the sea of people. Ryker is the VP of the Kings and one of the very few people in my life that I trust. It was him that introduced me to the Kings of Korruption in the first place. We'd met one night when he'd come into the bar I was working at. Some mouthy fuck had beaked off about my face, and I'd introduced him to the tread of my motorcycle boots. His buddies had jumped in and tried to take me out. That's when Ryker stepped in. Between the two of us, we'd kicked the shit out of every one of those mouthy sons-of-bitches, and I'd made my very first buddy.

I don't like the way he's looking at me right now, though. He looks pissed. I know that I sure as fuck didn't do anything to piss him off so I'm curious why he, and everyone else, is staring at me.

"'Bout fuckin' time ya got here. Been waitin' for over an hour," Ryker growls.

I cock my eyebrow, wondering what the fuck his point is. "Yeah? I was busy."

Ryker snorts. "Right. Well, nice of ya to make time for us." I don't say anything and just keep staring at him, waiting for him to make his point. He glares at me and shakes his head before giving it a jerk to indicate that I should follow him. Turning on his boot, he stalks out of the room. I follow behind him, eyeballing every nosey rubbernecker I can lay my eyes on. I'm just about out of the room when my eyes meet Mouse's. His are confused and a little worried as he shrugs his shoulders.

Like me, Mouse is a prospect. We don't often get invited into the meeting room of the Kings. As prospects, he and I spend a lot of time together doing one shitty task or another. In fact, I spend more time with Mouse than I do alone. Besides Ryker, Mouse is my only friend and the only other person in the world that I trust.

Why am I going into this meeting and not Mouse? What the fuck is going on? We enter the long rectangular room where we hold Church. Every patched member of the Kings of Korruption is sitting around it with their eyes on me as I enter behind Ryker. He moves directly to his seat, and I automatically head toward the tall stool situated in the back corner of the room. This is where prospects sit when they're invited to sit in on meetings.

Gunner Monroe clears his throat, causing all eyes, including my own, to turn to him. "All right! Let's get this fuckin' show on the road, shall we?" He bangs his fist down onto the table. His eyes lift to meet mine. He's trying to intimidate me, but I hold his stare. I won't lie, having Gunner stare you down is not a nice feeling, but he doesn't scare me. Nothing scares me anymore.

"As you all know, we have been here discussing the fate of our boy Tease." I sit up a little straighter and glance around the room, noting the glares I'm getting from everyone. "The time has come to decide if this crazy motherfucker deserves to wear our patch or not.

so we're gonna put it to a vote." My heartbeat picks up. This is it. I've been working my ass off for this for over a year. I'm older than most prospects and I haven't made many friends here, but I have been unfailingly loyal to every one of these cocksuckers. My skin heats with the attention that is focused on me, rage and nervousness churning slowly in my gut.

Ryker lifts his hand from the table. "I vote yeah." I nod my head at him in thanks and get a nod in return.

"I vote fuck yeah!" Jase.

"No." The word is growled from the fat fuck sitting next to Jase. Tiny sits at the table, eyes narrowed on me, shoulders squared in defiance. Everyone's eyes move to his, surprise held on many faces, but *I'm* not surprised. Tiny's had it out for me since the day I became a prospect.

Ryker's fist pounds down on the table. "For fuck's sake, Tiny! We fuckin' talked about this already. You fuckin' agreed!"

"Well, I changed my fuckin' mind, VP." His snarl is full of derision and contempt.

Ryker glares at Tiny but stays silent. It is against club laws to influence or sway the votes of any member. It also means I'm out. To be patched in, the vote has to be unanimous. My stomach drops. I'm done. Ever since I met Ryker, this club has been my life. *Now what the fuck do I do?*

I stand and raise my hands to remove my leather cut bearing the prospect patch. I feel like I'm in a trance, lost in a world that already fucking hates me. I thought I had finally found my place, but I was wrong once again.

Just as I fold up my cut to pass back to the club, a growl rips through the room. Reaper is on his feet, fists clenched at his sides. His face contorts in anger as he hollers out, "This is fuckin' bullshit! That fucker has done more for this club *today*, than you have done all fuckin' year, Tiny. What are you trying to fuckin' prove?"

"I ain't tryin' to prove shit. I just don't like the crazy prick. He's always just fuckin' lurkin' around the clubhouse and creepin' me the fuck out."

I stand frozen, rage attempting to consume me at his words. I *hate* his words. I want to cave his fucking face in for saying them. But instead, I move my eyes to Gunner, nod my head and place the cut on the stool I was sitting on. I turn and make a step to the door. I need to get the fuck out of here.

"Wait." Gunner is glaring daggers at Tiny. "Let's try this again. As we fuckin' discussed."

"Yes," Ryker states, anger consuming his features.

"Yes," Jase says through gritted teeth.

All eyes are locked on Tiny. He huffs out a breath and rolls his eyes. "Fuck. *Whatever*. Yes. Give the crazy fucker a patch. It'll do wonders for our already stellar repu-fucking-tation."

I continue to glare at him, hate fueling my every breath as the votes continue around the table, ending in a unanimous yes.

Jase lets out a whoop, breaking the tension in the room. "Put that fuckin' cut back on, brother! You can't get rid of us that easy!"

I look at him and shake my head. He's a nut too, just like Laynie. Disappointment takes over when her name enters my mind. I push it aside as I pull my cut back on and accept my new patch from Gunner. I will never have Laynie, but I finally *do* have a family. A real family that has my back. I watch as Tiny leaves the room while I endure back slaps and handshakes from the rest of the club. I'm going to have to keep an eye on that fucker.

Laynie

Do I call him? No, I don't want to seem too desperate. Why do I even want to call him? He was kind of a dick when I first talked to him. Yeah, but then he'd swooped in like a knight in leather armor, whisking me and my poor wounded dog to safety. Well, for the most part, anyway.

This is what happens when you drink wine alone — you talk to yourself. It's a good thing that I am a fabulous conversationalist then because I drink a lot of wine, and I always do it alone. Reaching over, I absently scratch Dexter's head. Well, not entirely alone – Dex has proven to be a great drinking buddy.

He lies beside me, curled up on the couch, his head in my lap as I contemplate one of the strangest most exciting encounters that I've ever had with a man. He must be hurting because usually he is off on the floor playing with his stuffed rabbit leaving me to drink all alone. I'm not a drunk; I just really like wine – a lot.

Finally, I can't take it anymore. The thought of never seeing Travis again makes my stomach churn. I *need* to call him. I need to hear his growly voice. Pressing the round button on the bottom of my iPhone, I instruct Siri to call Travis, praying that he didn't put his name in as Tease when he set it up.

The phone rings four times before someone answers. "Yeah?" His voice is so gruff and angry sounding. His lack of a proper greeting throws me off-guard.

I can't contain my giggle. "Yeah? That's how you answer your phone?"

Silence fills the other end of the line, but I can hear loud music and laughter in the background. "Laynie?" His voice is full of surprise.

"Uh-huh." Another giggle pours from my throat. I almost roll my own eyes. *Since when do I giggle?* Must be the booze.

"Are you drunk?"

"Yeppers. Wasted." Another giggle erupts, and I slap a hand over my mouth to contain it.

"Where are you?" he demands.

"At home. Me and Dexter are cuddled up on the couch, drinking a few bottles of wine." I pause, going back over my words. "Well, *Dexter's* not drinking wine. I am."

Amusement fills his voice when he asks, "How is Dexter, anyway?"

I sigh, reaching out to stroke Dex's fur. The truth is, he's lucky. It could have been so much worse. "He's OK. Just needs a couple days of rest." I swirl the glass in my hand, feeling the liquid sloshing around inside. Almost empty. For courage, I tip it back and down the remains of the glass.

"I nearly killed that fuckin' kid that hit him."

Heat floods me at the memory. He'd been so angry. Looking

back on it, his protectiveness was a major turn on. "I remember." Before I can stop the words, I say, "It was kind of hot." Embarrassment and excitement floods me, my heart pounding in my ears. I can't believe I just said that out loud. Time to change the subject and grab more wine for courage. I stand and head toward the kitchen.

"Anyway, I was thinking as a thank you, do you maybe want to—" Suddenly, I step on something soft, causing me to lift my foot quickly and attempt to change course. My body stumbles to the side, and my shin painfully catches the end table beside the couch. Something falls to the floor, landing and shattering just as my body lands amongst the pieces. Pain sears through my shin and the heel of my foot. "Ow! Shit!"

I sit there, in a daze for a moment until I hear Travis's disembodied voice coming from my phone somewhere off to the left. "Laynie? What the fuck was that?"

All pain forgotten, I scramble around wildly, hands skimming the hard wood flooring back and forth in an attempt to locate my likely shattered iPhone. I can hear the question in his voice, so I call out, "Hello? Travis?" I listen for him to call out to me again and keep searching, but I can't seem to find it anywhere. "Shit! I dropped the phone."

Worried that he will get annoyed and hang up, I call out to my savior. "Dexter! Get your drunk ass over here and help Mommy find her phone." I feel bad asking him to get up on his sore leg and look for it, but Travis is going to hang up before I can ask him to stop by. I need to get that question out there. I need to see him again.

His tiny voice calls out again. "Laynie?"

I hear Dexter moving around, nose sniffing out my lost phone. "That's it, baby. Find Mommy's phone." His dog tags jingle as he roots around on the floor for another moment, and then he's in front of me, placing the phone on my outstretched hand. "That's my good boy. Thank you, baby."

I quickly pull the phone up to my ear before I notice the slime. "Ugh! Gross! Now there's slobber all over it." Wrinkling my nose in disgust, I quickly wipe my slimed phone and hand on my pant leg before lifting it back to my ear once again. "Travis? You there?"

"I'm here." He sounds amused, and I can't help but smile.

"Sorry. I dropped my phone." Realizing he is well aware that I dropped my phone, I giggle again. I'm really showing him what a great catch I am. For just a fraction of a moment, I regret being drunk while I make this call.

"What was that crash?" The background noise on his end dims slightly.

"Just the table." A hiccup rocks my chest, loud and harsh.

"What broke?"

I look around as if I can see to answer his question. *Nope. Still black.* "Something on the table?"

"You don't know what that something was?"

My nose scrunches up in confusion. *What's his problem?* "Travis, I'm blind. I've got no clue what the hell it was."

He chuckles softly which is my new favorite sound. I hear murmurs and then laughter from the other end, but I can't make out what they're saying. Realizing that he's likely still dealing with his "work shit", I feel like an idiot. A drunken idiot that calls a completely sexy sounding man while he's busy and spends most of the phone call flailing around on the floor, yelling at her dog like a total fucking lunatic. I awkwardly get to my feet and open my mouth to let him get back to his party, but before I can get the words out, pain slices through my foot causing me to cry out loudly. *Shit. That fucking hurts.*

"Laynie? You OK?" He sounds almost panicked all of the sudden, and I turn my body slightly, flopping back down on the couch, embarrassed.

My cheeks flame as I search my brain for an answer. "Um. Yeah?" Another hiccup sneaks past my lips. I try my best to sound sober and pain free. "I'll be fine." I fail even to my own ears. The slurred speech may give me away.

"You don't *sound* fine." *He* sounds annoyed. *What else is new?*

"I just stepped on glass or something. I'll be fine." Waving my hand dismissively, I attempt to end this disastrous conversation. "Anyways, I won't keep you. I just wanted to invite you over for dinner tomorrow. Or this week. Or whenever." *God, Laynie. Shut up!*

"You bleedin'?"

Confusion causes a frown to crease my forehead. *Didn't he hear my question?* "What?"

"Your foot. You bleedin'?"

I shake my head slightly before tilting it down toward my feet. "Uh. Yeah. I think so." Reaching down, I gently run my fingertips over my throbbing heel. Pain rips through me as I graze a large piece of glass, embedded deep into my flesh. "Ahh! Yep." I nod my head and take a deep breath, gritting my teeth through the pain. My fingertips come away wet. "Definitely bleeding."

"Be there in ten."

I bolt upright in my seat, the pain suddenly forgotten. I don't want that. I want to see him, but I don't want him to come over because I'm a drunken mess who tried to slice her foot in half on an unidentified object.

"No! Travis, I'm fine. I'll just —"

"I said I'll be there in ten. Sit your ass down, and don't move."

And there he was. Coffee Dick. "Travis! Don't you dare talk to me li–"

"Can't talk to you and drive my bike, babe."

My eyes narrow. "Travis–"

"Say what you gotta say in ten minutes. Sit tight."

The line goes dead before I even get a chance to think about what to say to that. Somewhere between the first and the fourth glass of wine, I'd forgotten what an asshole he can be. I stab at the bottom button on my phone fiercely to activate Siri and direct her to phone Travis.

The phone rings and rings. No voicemail picks up so I continue to let it ring, knowing damn well that he can hear it. I scream out loudly in frustration before turning it off, tossing the phone onto the couch, and slumping back into the cushions with a dramatic sigh.

My foot throbs. *I can't believe that asshole hung up on me!* Then I remember what he said at the end. *Ten minutes!* I can't look sexy in ten minutes! I'm wearing flannel pajamas, for fuck's sake! Regardless, he'll be here no matter what so I better get to work.

Jumping off the couch, I hop on one foot all the way to the bathroom so I can at least fix my hair and put on some lip gloss. It's not until I am smearing the cherry-flavored goo on my lips that I wonder out loud, "How the hell does he know where I live?"

Tease

AFTER FINDING A spot to park my bike on the narrow residential street, I rush up to the door of Laynie's apartment building. Beside it hangs a panel with four buttons, each showing a last name and apartment number. I have no fucking idea what Laynie's last name is, nor do I know which apartment is hers, but thanks to my new side hobby as a fucking stalker, I do know that this is her building.

"Fuck!" I stab at the first button. No answer. I stab at the second button.

A man's disembodied voice comes from the speaker. "Hello?"

"I'm looking for Laynie."

The speaker is silent for a moment before he comes back on. "Who's this?"

I grit my teeth and answer. "A friend. It's a fuckin' emergency!" The thought of Laynie inside hurt and bleeding makes me feel like I'm coming out of my fucking skin. I eyeball the door, looking for the quickest way to break the goddamned lock.

Silence from the speaker causes my chest to feel heavy with tension before it finally comes to life again. "Straight up the stairs and it's the first door on the right." The door buzzes, unlatching when I yank on it.

Although I'm thankful that he let me in, anger flows through me as I enter the building, wondering what kind of jackass just lets a complete stranger into the locked building of a beautiful woman and tells them exactly where to find her. That shit is going to be dealt with.

Stepping up to the door, I raise my hand and knock loudly, calling out, "Laynie?"

From inside, I hear a muffled voice, and then the door is pulled open. Rushing inside, I see Laynie sitting on the couch, a glass of wine clutched in her hand.

"You hung up on me!" I ignore her and hurry to the couch, crouching down to check her over for injuries. "That wasn't very nice, Travis."

I look up from where I was checking her over, spearing her eyes with my own. They are the greenest eyes I've ever seen. "I ain't nice."

She snorts and rolls her eyes. "I'm learning that." She lifts her glass and takes a swallow of wine. It's then I realize that someone else had opened the door. Standing quickly, I whip back around. Dexter stands in front of the closed door, long tongue hanging out as he grins goofily up at me. My eyes move to the door knob, which is actually a handle with a long cloth tied to it.

"Your fucking dog answered the door."

From her place on the couch, Laynie laughs lightly. "I know. I told him to."

I turn back to her. "That is very fucking cool."

She grins her wonky grin causing my heart to thud in my chest. *What the fuck is wrong with me?* And then I see the blood. All over the hardwood floor is several trails of smeared blood. Squatting back down in front of her, I grab her feet and look for the source of her bleeding. "Fuck, babe. I told you to fuckin' sit still."

She shrugs and drains what's left of her wine before wagging the empty glass at me. "I was thirsty."

I shake my head and lift her foot to inspect the damage. Hissing through my teeth, I see several small shards of glass embedded in the skin, surrounding a large chunk buried deep in her heel. "Fuck. That looks like it hurts."

I glance up and meet her eyes, my breath catching in my chest. They are so green. It's like she's looking right at me, and for a brief moment, I forget that she can't see. Standing, I scoop her off the couch and start walking toward the hallway.

She squeals and giggles, wiggling as she shouts, "Travis! Put me down! Where are you taking me?"

"You got a first-aid kit in the bathroom?"

She sighs and stops squirming, leaning back into my arms, the wide smile still on her face. "Yes, Father. In the medicine cabinet above the sink."

Shaking my head, I give her a squeeze and growl. "Don't be a smartass."

We enter the bathroom as she shrugs. "It's who I am. Deal with it."

Smirking, I place her gently on the counter beside the sink. After locating the first aid kit, I open it up and kneel in front of her, holding her foot up to the light. "Gonna clean this up as best as I can, babe, but you likely need stitches."

Her lower lip pops out in a childish pout. "No hospital. Just slap a Band-Aid on it, and I'll be fine."

I don't think a fucking Band-Aid is what she needs, but I set to work cleaning it up. Using a pair a tweezers, I carefully remove the tiny pieces of glass embedded in her skin. Every time she cries out, my fucking heart squeezes. I hate that I'm hurting her, but I continue, hands shaking like a goddamned pussy in my attempt to be gentle. When I'm done, her foot is cleaned, disinfected and bandaged. It wasn't as bad as it had looked at first.

I stand from my crouch, and for the first time, I notice what she's wearing. A tight green camisole clings to her rounded breasts, her nipples showing slightly through the material. I can't take my eyes off of them. If I were to lean forward just a few inches, I could pull one of those tight buds between my lips, and fuck *me*, do I want to. After a few seconds pass, I realize that I'm just standing there like an asshole, staring at her tits while my cock presses harder and harder against my zipper.

Reaching down, I readjust my dick and clear my throat. "Done." My voice is husky with need, and I know she can hear it. Looking back at her, I see that though she may have heard it, in her drunken haze she didn't catch it. She just sits there smiling, eyes half-closed, looking like she is about to pass the fuck out.

"Babe? You good?"

She smiles a small wine-induced smile. "Hmmm. Sleepy."

There's no way in hell she's making it back to the couch tonight. Shaking my head, I scoop her up once more and carry her out into the hallway. Looking around, I see only one other open door. Deciding that must be the bedroom, I turn and move in that direction.

Her head rests on my shoulder, her hand on my chest, and her strawberry smell fills my nostrils, doing very little to tame my raging hard on. The fact that the smell of fruit turns me on makes me question my own fucking sanity, but I know that it's the smell of her that is causing the blood to rush straight to my dick. This woman is the sexiest thing I've ever seen.

I'm just entering the bedroom when she lifts up slightly and buries her nose in my neck. Her hand on my chest presses harder and starts to stroke across the muscles there. "Mmm. You smell good. And your chest feels like iron. Soft, sexy, iron."

Fuck. I need to get the hell out of here. Hurrying over to the bed, I gently place her on top, her head on the pillow. "Get some sleep. You're gonna feel like shit in the mornin'."

Her sleepy smile grows, even with her eyes closed. "Aww, Travis. *See.* You *are* nice."

Warmth washes over me. *What is it with this woman?* I wish she were right. I wish I were nice, but I'm not — I'm a fucking monster.

"Night, Laynie." My voice is harsh and angry sounding, but my heart is pounding rapidly in my chest. This sweet woman is fucking with my head.

Rolling to her side, she calls out, "Travis?"

I pause in my retreat through the door. "Yeah."

"Thank you for fixing my foot." Her words are slow and calculated, and I know she's struggling to stay awake. "You're a...just...thanks."

I stand in front of her watching her sweet face and wonder what the fuck to do now. Her eyes fall closed, and her smile slowly fades. She's asleep. Part of me knows that I need to leave. I need to get away from her and never fucking come back. I don't know why I came in the first place. I don't want any type of relationship – with her or with anyone. I could never trust her, and the thought of Laynie betraying me like everyone else has makes my fucking gut twist.

But I do know why I came. She was hurt – I couldn't *not* come. Just the thought of her hurting and alone was enough to make me hop on my bike and fly to her rescue, like a fucking pussy-whipped bitch. Watching her now, I worry.

What if she gets up in the night and hurts herself again? She's wasted. I can't leave her. Shoulders slumped in defeat, I walk from her bedroom to the living room. Dexter stands by the doorway, leash in his mouth, obviously needing to go outside. *The dog's as crazy as his master.*

Running my hand down my face, I sigh heavily before taking the leash from the dog. "All right, buddy. Let's go."

Clipping the leash onto his collar, I take the fucking dog out.

Laynie

The overwhelming need to pee slowly pulls me from my sleep. Groggily, I bury my face deeper into the pillow and groan. I feel like shit. My head throbs, my body aches, and my mouth tastes terrible. Feeling wetness on my cheek, I lift my head and touch the pillow. *Gross.* Drool.

Sliding my hand along my chin to wipe the excess from my skin, I yawn and stretch, trying to wake myself up. My brain is fuzzy as I try to remember what the hell I did last night. Reaching out, I pat the air intending to pat Dex. He likely hates me right now. I don't remember taking him out to pee last night at all.

My hand searches the blankets beside me but comes up with

nothing but air. Dex isn't there. *Weird.* "Dex." My call is barely more than a whisper thanks to my dry throat. Hearing a noise from the kitchen, I bolt upright in bed.

"Dex!" My voice is louder this time, and my heart pounds in my chest as I wait to hear something from the other room – anything. Suddenly, I hear the tinkling of Dex's dog tags coming closer, followed by the heavy thump of footsteps. Fear causes my blood to run cold.

"Hello?" The door squeaks quietly as it's pushed open, and suddenly Dex is on the bed, his wet nose pushing into my hand. I reach up and give him a stroke, straining my ears for the sounds of footsteps. Slowly, I lean toward my nightstand, feeling for the large paper weight I keep there. It's not much of a weapon, but it could cause a serious headache if it were to crash its way into the skull of an unwelcome houseguest. "Who's there?"

"Just me."

Relief floods me when I realize that it's Travis, but is quickly replaced with confusion then embarrassment as the events of the night before come flooding back to me. *Oh God.* My drunk dialing him had not been my wisest move. And topping it off with slicing my foot open was classic. *Way to show him what a great catch you are, dumbass.*

Groaning, I bury my face in my hands. "Oh God. I'm such an idiot."

His footsteps approach the bed. "I made you breakfast. Your foot's gonna be sore for a few days, so you need to stay off it."

I sink my head lower into my hands, and my words are muffled. "Thank you. I'm so freaking embarrassed."

An amused snort fills my ears, coming from closer than he was before. "Babe, it's cool."

It dawns on me then that it's morning, and he's still here. "You stayed the night?"

He inhales heavily. "Yeah, well, I wanted to make sure you didn't get up in the night and fall again."

Anger creeps its way into my thoughts making my cheeks flush with heat. I have to work to control my voice. "Cause I'm blind?"

Annoyance clear in his voice, he replies, "No, because you were flat on your ass drunk with glass sticking out of your fuckin' foot." As quickly as it came, the anger washes away with relief at his honest answer. "I slept on the couch, took the dog out, made you breakfast – you need to eat. It'll get rid of that hangover."

My cheeks flame brighter. *He slept on my couch?* I may not be able to see him, but I've felt him...kind of. And his voice comes from high above me when we're standing. I know he's tall, so I don't know how he fit on my short, flowery couch.

"Well...thank you for staying. And for the breakfast and dealing with Dex." An awkward vibe fills the room, and I search my mind frantically for something to say, but he beats me to it.

"Yeah." The awkward silence remains until he breaks it with his gruff voice. "Look, I gotta go. Get some food into you, and stay off your foot for a while." His footsteps moving toward the door and my heart pounds. I need to say something – anything.

"Travis?"

His steps pause, but he says nothing.

"I'm making stuffed manicotti for supper tonight. Did you want to join me?" Silence fills the air, its weight choking me. "I always make too much and can never eat it all myself."

"Not a good idea," he grunts.

His attitude is starting to piss me off. "Yeah. Maybe you're right." I clench my jaw and try my best to glare in his direction. "I mean, who knows which one of your personalities is going to show up."

Silence.

I sigh heavily and force the emotion from my voice, doing my best to sound dismissive. "Thanks again for helping me out last night, Travis. I didn't need it, but thanks anyways. Now, if you don't mind, I need to use the little girl's room, so you'll have to show yourself out."

More silence. I'm beginning to wonder if he'd managed to leave without me noticing when he speaks again. "What's stuffed manicotti?"

I can't help the smirk. He always sounds so angry, but I'm beginning to wonder if that's just his normal tone. "It's noodle tubes stuffed with different cheeses and smothered in a sausage and tomato sauce."

More silence, broken only by the sound of his feet shuffling. "What time?"

Excitement fills me – butterflies swarming in my belly – but I keep the cool tone in my words. "Seven thirty?"

He grunts, "I'll be here."

Still sitting on my bed, my hand on Dex's back, I listen to Travis walk through my apartment and out the front door. The feeling of triumph freezes me in place, my face split in a wide and gleeful grin. Apparently food really *is* the way to a man's heart.

I jump from my bed about to do a victory dance. Just as my foot hits the floor, pain sears through my wounded heel. "Ow! Shit!"

Abandoning my victory dance, my heart soars with excitement as I limp my way to the bathroom.

Tease

CLOSING THE DOOR to Laynie's apartment, I'm just about to move to the main door of the building when the door across the hall opens. A young guy, about twenty-five, steps out and freezes when he sees me. He glances from me to Laynie's door several times and swallows hard.

"You the guy that let me in last night?"

His eyes locked on mine, he nods. The guy's terrified.

"You do that often?"

Eyes still wide, he shakes his head no.

I take a few steps toward him, causing him to step back and press himself against his apartment door. "I ever hear of you letting another stranger into this fuckin' building and tellin' 'em where to find Laynie, I'll rip your fuckin' heart out. Got me?"

He stays pressed against the wall and says nothing as he nods. Holding his stare for a moment, I glare at him, showing him just how fucking serious I am before turning and stalking out of the building and down the street to my ride.

My phone chimes with a text just as I'm about to swing my leg over. Yanking it from the back pocket of my jeans, I see that it's

Gunner.

Gunner: 911. Church in 30.

A small rush of pride fills me as I realize that he's added me to the group list of patched members. After years of wandering this fucked up world on my own, I finally belong somewhere. Glancing back at Laynie's building, I grit my teeth. *Why did I agree to come back for dinner?* I may belong to the club, but I don't belong in that girly fucking apartment with that woman. I need to cancel. I should never have agreed in the first fucking place.

The drive to the clubhouse is short, and I pull in beside Jase just as he's getting off his ride. He stops, waiting for me to get off my own. "Where the fuck did you take off to last night, Romeo? You got some pussy on the side you ain't sharin' with the rest of us?"

I shoulder my way past him, giving him a warning glare as I do. He laughs out loud and follows along behind me. "Oh, secret pussy. I hear ya, bro. Secret pussy is my favorite *kind* of pussy."

I spin around, stopping him in his tracks. "It's none of your fuckin' business where I went. And I don't want to hear about your fuckin' pussy."

As I turn and start strolling toward the clubhouse once again, Jase laughs. "All right, brother. I hear ya. No more pussy. You did miss a hell of a party after you left last night, though. Lucy was looking for you too. Wanted to give you a welcome to the club present. She gives it to all the new brothers."

I curl my nose at the thought of that nasty bitch touching me. Sure, I'd fucked her a couple of times, but I'd never let her touch me, and I'd never touched her more than I had to. Jase snickers at my expression, and we enter the clubhouse. The common room is cleaned up, floors and tables gleaming. You'd never know there was a party there the night before. The old ladies of the club have been busy this morning.

The meeting room is full, a brother sitting at every available seat at the long oval table. The only seats left are Jase's, and what looks to be my newly appointed seat, directly between him and Reaper. We enter the room and take our seats quietly, waiting for the Prez to tell us what the fuck is so important.

Gunner clears his throat and sits forward in his chair. "I called you all here today because we have a situation. Ryk, this one affects you the most." Ryker's frame goes still as he waits for Gunner to continue. "That sick fuck, Krueger, was killed last night in prison."

Shock fills the room. It's not like we care – Krueger had it coming. He'd gone rogue from the Devil's Rejects MC and kidnapped Ryker's woman. He almost fucking killed her. He's lucky he lived this long. I don't know how Ryker didn't kill him in the first place; I'd have turned that fucker inside out.

Gunner looks around the table, letting it sink in. "I, for one, am glad the fucker's dead. The problem, though, is that the Devils think we had something to do with it. Think we went back on our agreement to let them question him about some shit they have goin' on in their *own* club."

The room fills with voices all speaking at the same time. I stay silent watching Ryker. He says nothing, but his face is filled with fury. I know he had nothing to do with it. He wanted to kill that son-of-a-bitch himself, and had been working out a way to do it.

Gunner bangs his gavel on the table. "Quiet!" Everyone stops talking, restless energy pulsating throughout the room. "The Devils are pissed. They think we killed him before they got a chance to get what they needed from him. I told them we had nothin' to do with it, but they are convinced it was Ryker."

Ryker clenches his fists, his jaw hardening. I know he *wishes* that it was. Not getting to kill that son-of-a-bitch himself is gonna haunt the poor bastard for the rest of his life.

"The Devil's Prez told me that killing Krueger was an act of war." The room swells with outraged shouts and a jumble of angry protests. "I couldn't convince the stupid bastard that it wasn't us, or our boy here, so I wanted you all to be aware. The Devils *will* retaliate – it isn't gonna be fuckin' pretty. Keep your eyes peeled and stay alert. Nobody moves anywhere without carryin' your piece and keep it loaded at all times." Gunner leans forward and spears each of us with his fierce, green eyes. "We are officially at war, boys. Stay safe."

He bangs his gavel once more, officially ending the meeting. One by one, the brothers stand, anger fueling every conversation. I stand slowly, making my way to Ryker. He looks up from his seat, eyes dark and furious. Holding my fist out to him, I say, "Whatever you need, brother."

Gritting his teeth, he just nods, bumping his fist into mine.

I get it. I know what it's like to have rage buried so deep inside you that you can't speak. To be so enraged that you fear opening your mouth will lead to insanity. Being that angry is how I've lived my life for the last twenty years. Giving him a chin lift, I turn and head out the door.

Just as I swing my leg over my bike, Mouse comes running up behind me. "Tease! I need to talk to you."

I cut my eyes to his, waiting for him to say more.

"I met this girl —" I don't even wait for him to finish. Mouse and his fucking women. The guy is only nineteen and seems to think every girl he meets is going to be "the one". Then they turn out to be complete trash, and it just about breaks him every time. For the first time ever, I've got my own fucking women troubles – I don't need to hear about his.

"No! Wait!" I turn back and stare at him again. "This one's different. I've been seeing her for a while now. She told me this morning…" He runs his fingers through his hair, body twitching with excitement. "She's fuckin' pregnant, dude. I'm gonna be a fuckin' daddy!"

I don't know what to say. If some bitch told me I was going to be a dad, I'd lose my fucking shit. "Fuck."

"No, man. It's cool! I'm gonna be a fuckin' daddy!" He grins at me, his whole face splitting wide with happiness.

I can't relate. Being a father sounds like my idea of a fucking nightmare. Mouse will be a good dad, though. He may be just a kid, but he's a good person – always happy, and he would give you the shirt off his back if you asked for it. If he's happy about it, well, good for him. I don't know why the fuck he came to *me* about it, though. Sure, we've spent a lot of time together as prospects, but if he hasn't learned by now that I don't participate in his whacked out conversations, he never will.

I give him the best response I can come up with. "Good for you, Mouse." He beams at me and opens his mouth to say more, but I start the motor up on my bike, revving it loudly before I peel out of the parking lot. Mouse can figure out his own shit. I have things to do today, and the first on the list is calling Laynie to cancel this fucking dinner.

Laynie

I hadn't even finished my breakfast yet when the phone calls start. Knowing it's my mother, I finish eating and put my plate in the dishwasher, letting it ring. In the time it takes me to have a shower and fix my hair, she's called three more times. With each ring of the phone, my anger builds. The fifth time she calls, I answer it.

"Hello, Mom." I know she can hear my annoyance — I don't even try to hide it.

"Well, it's about time! I've been trying to get ahold of you all morning."

"I know. I was busy."

"Too busy to answer the phone when your mother calls?"

Gritting my teeth, I make an effort to remind myself that matricide is illegal and that this is my mother, and I love her. "What can I do for you, Mom?"

She lets out an exaggerated sigh, making my annoyance turn to outright aggravation. "Daniel is coming home tonight for the weekend. Are you still coming with him?"

Crap! I'd forgotten all about that. "Uh…actually, no. I —"

"No? What do you mean no? You and Daniel come home the second weekend of every month! It's a tradition."

I want to scream at her. Tell her to leave me the hell alone and to back the fuck off – but I don't. "I know. It's just something has come up. I uh …. I have a date."

Silence. "A date?" Why does she sound like I just told her I wanted to run off to the Arctic to become a fucking penguin?

"Yes, a date! I have those from time to time!" I can't believe her.

It's like she thinks nobody would ever want a date with me just because I'm blind.

"Well, who is this boy? What does he do?"

What *does* he do? "He's not a boy, Mom. He's a man. I don't know how old he is, but I think he's around my age. And I don't know what he does."

"Don't know! Laynie! You can't go on a date with a strange man! Honey…what are you thinking?"

Aggravation is lost to full-on anger. "I'm thinking that this is the first guy in a long time that doesn't treat me like a fucking cripple! I'm thinking that he's a good person! I'm thinking that my own mother should know me well enough to trust my judgment. And I'm thinking that I need to get off of this phone before I say something I'm going to regret."

"Laynie Marie! Don't you take that t —"

"Goodbye, Mom."

I disconnect the call and flop down onto the couch. *God! She is so infuriating!* Before my accident, my mom and I were close. My whole family was close. I don't know if it was losing Garrett or me losing my sight that's made her into the neurotic "momster" that she is, but I can't take it anymore.

I've put up with it for nine years now, and she'll be lucky to survive it until ten. I don't know how my dad puts up with her. I guess it's because he spends most of his time in the garage just to get away from her special brand of crazy. I moved to Ottawa to get away from her myself. I needed to escape. I wanted to go to Toronto, but Daniel lives here, and it was a compromise I agreed to avoid giving her an early stroke. Plus, I love my brother. I like having the opportunity to spend time with him without my mother hovering like a low-flying helicopter.

After texting my brother to let him know I'm not coming with him tonight, I decide I need an escape. Remembering the new book I'm set to review, I decide to spend the morning listening to it and lose myself in the world of hot bikers and their bitches. Reading has always been an escape for me and with audio books becoming more and more popular, it has made my life so much easier.

I make myself a cup of coffee, put on my earphones and curl up under my favorite blanket, letting my newest book boyfriend sweep me off my feet.

Laynie

TRAVIS IS LATE. He was supposed to be here forty-five minutes ago, and I'm beginning to think he's not coming. Disappointment causes my heart to feel heavy. I'd spent the entire day nursing my hangover, cleaning my apartment, and cooking this meal. I'd worked hard on it. I wanted to make it perfect for him as my way of thanking the cranky son-of-a-bitch for all of his help. Now, looking back, I don't even know why I'd invited him. He barely speaks, and when he does it's more like a growl. He'd turned down my invitation at first, and I hadn't pushed so why the hell had he accepted if he wasn't even going to have the decency to show up?

Shaking my head, I drain my first of many glasses of wine and wander to the counter so I can wrap the baked dish in foil. Might as well put it in the fridge and use it for the next few nights. Good thing I love manicotti. I empty the last of one bottle of wine into my glass and am just trying to decide whether the three bottles I have left is enough or if I need to walk to the liquor store when the door buzzer sounds.

My belly erupts in a storm of flutters and my heart pounds with excitement. *He did come.* Hurrying over to the buzzer, only stubbing my toe once on the way, I press the bottom button and make an effort to sound uninterested. "Hello?"

The thirty seconds it takes for him to answer feels like a year. "It's Travis." My excitement fades a little. He doesn't sound happy to be here at all.

I press the button to let him in, not responding. Turning from the wall-mounted buzzer, I quickly pinch my cheeks and rearrange my breasts. "All right, Dex. How do I look?"

Dex doesn't answer, but he does come and stand beside me while we wait for the knock on the door. When it comes, I call out, "Coming!" and proceed to stand there a little longer. I don't want him to think I'm too eager, and besides, he's very late. Let *him* wait for *me* now.

After a minute, Dex gives me a nudge. Figuring he'd waited long enough, I walk casually to the door and open it wide, schooling my features to be free of any emotion. "Hello, Travis."

"Hey." Silence surrounds us once again. "Drinkin' again?"

I arch my brow and hold up my glass. "Yep, and I'm just about ready for a top up." I take a step back, allowing him to follow me inside. I hear the sounds of Dex's collar jingling as Travis greets him. "You're late."

The jingling stops. "I am." He's closer now. I can feel the heat from his body and his breath on my cheek. "I wasn't going to come."

My breath catches. "Why did you?"

"Because you wouldn't answer the phone when I tried to cancel."

The disappointment I'd felt earlier returns. "I had my phone off. My mother was driving me up the wall." Taking a sip of my wine, I motion toward the door. "You can go if you want to."

"No. I can't."

I frown. "Why not?"

"Cause that shit smells fuckin' delicious, and I'm starving."

"You're right. It does." I put one hand on my hip and point my glass toward the kitchen. "That's because I spent all afternoon getting it ready." I turn and head for the kitchen. "I already put it in the fridge, since I assumed you weren't coming, but I guess I can get it

44

back out and heat you up a plate."

I hear him following me and am instantly self-conscious of the table setting I had made. I'd set this up just like a date. The table is set neatly with linen napkins and a trio of pillar candles in the center. He didn't come here for a date. He came here to eat, and because I didn't answer the phone so he could cancel.

Hoping to distract him from my obviously misguided assumption, I reach into the fridge and pull out another bottle of wine. I turn toward him and hold it out. "Would you like a glass of wine?"

"Not a fuckin' chance. Would love a beer, though."

Beer? Why the hell didn't I think of beer? "Uh…let me check." I turn, rustling around at the back of the fridge, pulling out a beer like I'd just found a diamond. "Ha! I knew Daniel left some here!" I twist the cap off and hold it out to him.

He doesn't take it. "Daniel?" he growls.

"Yeah. My brother."

He gently pulls the beer from my hand. "Thanks."

Was he jealous there for a minute? Or is that just wishful thinking? Turning back to the fridge, I set about getting supper ready again. Once everything is dished up and heated, I bring it all to the table. Cheeks flaming with embarrassment, I set it down. "We can move to the living room if you'd like."

"This is fine." His voice is gruff, but I'm slowly learning that this is just the way he is and it doesn't necessarily mean he's angry. Travis is a man of few words. He reminds me so much of the kids I work with – a little broken and needing some subtle motivation to put himself back together.

Nodding, I take my seat and another long gulp of wine. This is so awkward. It wouldn't be so bad if he wanted to be here, but his demeanor and his lateness tell me he doesn't, and I feel like an ass. I don't even know this guy. *What am I doing?*

Tease

This is a date. The fucking table has candles on it. I can tell just by looking at it and the way she's dressed that she thought it was. I don't fucking date, and I don't know why I didn't accept her offer to move to the living room. Maybe it was the way her hair was shining in the candle light, or the embarrassed expression on her face when she led me into the kitchen. It could have been the jealous feeling that took over when she pulled a beer from the fridge claiming that *Daniel* had left it here. I know she's pissed that I was so late, and I don't fucking blame her. She'd put some serious effort into this meal. Too bad she's wasting it on me.

I feel like a total asshole. "Laynie?"

She jumps a little as if startled from her thoughts. "Yeah?"

What the fuck do I say? I don't know if I've apologized to anyone since I was a little kid. "I'm sorry I was late. It was a dick move."

"You? A dick? Never." She smirks, eyebrow raised slightly.

A snort of amusement escapes before I can stop it. "Smartass."

She sighs then and puts down her glass. "Whatever. You're here now. Let's just eat." After a few minutes of silence, she clears her throat and takes a bite of her pasta. "So...did you get your work shit taken care of yesterday?'

I pause. I know she's only trying to make conversation, but I don't want to share anything with her. Sharing shit with anyone has always resulted in getting knifed in the back. I can't trust her — I can't trust *anyone*.

Her green eyes are focused slightly to the left as she waits for my answer, innocence clear on her face. I've already hurt her feelings tonight, and that doesn't sit well with me for some reason. The least I can do is attempt to fucking talk to her.

"Yep."

She chuckles. "Did you work today?"

"I work every day."

I watch as she nibbles on her bottom lip. "I only work Monday to Friday for a few hours in the morning. It's a sweet deal. The rest of the time, I blog."

"Blog?" *What the fuck is a blog?*

"Yeah. I read, and I have a blog about reading and books. It's really fun, and I've made a ton of friends online."

"Online." I think about that. "How does that work exactly? Reading and using a computer?"

She smiles. "Since Apple products became more popular, my life has gotten so much better. I use a computer with a voiceover option. My phone and e-reader have the same thing. And I listen to a lot of audiobooks instead of actually reading."

I nod, only understanding part of what the hell she's talking about. I don't use computers at all. I only even have a cell phone because Gunner said I had to get one. Curious about her, I ask another question. "What do you do in the mornings?"

"For my other job?" I nod, even though she can't see me. "I work as a Vision Loss Counsellor at the children's hospital."

Admiration for her washes over me. "You work with blind kids?"

"Yep. Sometimes, when they become blind, people have a hard time letting go of the idea of being sighted. I help them embrace themselves as they are. They need to learn that they can still have an incredible life without vision."

The way she talks about being blind like it's no big deal floors me. And using it to help others? *Who is this woman?* I've never met anyone like her.

"What do you do for a living, Travis?"

I snort. "Well, I ain't savin' blind kids from themselves, that's for sure." She says nothing while she finishes the last of her meal. I look around the room at her frilly apartment and wonder once again what the hell I'm doing here. To an outsider, we would look like a fucking modern day Beauty and The Beast. She needs to know who I am.

"I'm a biker."

Her head tilts slightly to the side, a small line forming between her eyebrows. "OK. A biker. I already knew you rode. I can smell it on you."

"An outlaw biker. One of the Kings of Korruption." I take a swig of my beer and watch her face for any reaction, but she gives away nothing. Any second now, I know she's going to freak the fuck out and kick my ass out of here.

Her face breaks out into her wonky grin, eyes shining brightly in the candlelight. "Now that is the sexiest fucking thing I have ever heard."

I choke. Beer shoots from my lips and my nostrils burn. "What?"

She giggles. "I told you...I read a lot. Biker books are the sexiest books I've ever read. I thought you were going to say you were a mechanic or something. Biker is way better." That wonky grin returns to her face and I can't help it – I chuckle, knowing full-well that her biker books and my biker world are not even close to the same thing.

"You're a fuckin' nut, you know that?"

She laughs, the sound of it filling my ears and settling somewhere deep inside my battered soul. Standing, she takes my plate and hers to the kitchen and offers me another beer. I was going to leave as soon as we finished eating, but I can't bring myself to go. I want to know more about her. I want to know what she'll say next.

With a full beer and a fresh glass of wine, we move to the living room and sit side by side on the couch. I think about her job and wonder how she does it. How can she live her life so happily after having that shit handed to her? I may not be blind, but the night I got my scar, I changed forever. It's turned me into the monster I am. I *had* to become that to protect myself.

"Have you always been blind?" The question escapes my lips before I can stop it, and I think it takes us both off-guard.

She turns to face me and tilts her head to the side. "No, actually. I lost my sight when I was seventeen." She smiles wistfully and takes a small sip of wine. Silently, I wait for her to continue. "My older brother, Garrett, was only eleven months older than me, and we were really close."

My heart clenches. I already have a sense of where this story is going, and I can tell by the sadness on her face that she's going to tell me something that will hurt her to tell.

"It was prom night, and Garrett was driving. We'd just dropped off the last of our friends and were making our way home when Journey came on the radio." A tear slips down her cheek. "'Don't Stop Believin'." Her wobbly smile punches me right in the chest. "It was one of our favorite songs. We used to do a wicked duet to it. Garrett cranked it up, and we were singing like a pair of idiots when a drunk driver crossed the yellow line and hit us head on."

More tears start to flow, and she takes a deep breath. I can't stand watching her struggle like this, but I have no fucking clue what to say. As she takes a fortifying sip of wine, I place my hand on her knee, offering her whatever support I can as she finishes her story.

"I smashed my head in the collision and suffered severe optic nerve damage. I'll likely never see again." She places her hand on mine, giving it a squeeze. "I'm lucky, though, really. I'm still here. Garrett wasn't so lucky. He died on impact."

I squeeze her hand back, heart heavy with an emotion I can't explain.

"We were in that car for two hours before someone found us."

"You're so fucking brave." The words come out like a growl, thanks to the gigantic lump in my throat, but I fucking mean them. How she can sit in front of me with a smile on her face and tell me that fucking story is a goddamned mystery to me.

She smiles softly. "Not really. Just a survivor. Anyone can be a survivor with the right attitude."

I don't like how she's downplaying it. She's a fucking miracle, and she won't acknowledge it. Turning my body toward hers, I squeeze her hand tightly and place my other hand around the side of her neck. "That may be true, but not everyone can be a fuckin' inspiration to so many people. You are. Don't dismiss that shit."

My eyes are boring into hers, waiting to see if she is listening to what I'm saying, so I'm caught off-guard when she grins. "You told me that you aren't nice, but you never told me that you're sweet."

I stiffen and squeeze her neck, growling, "I ain't fuckin' sweet."

She laughs out loud, the joy on her face breathtaking. "I hate to tell you, tough guy, you work hard at hiding it, but you are."

Gritting my teeth, I remove my hand and move to stand up, but her hand on my arm stops me. "Thank you, Travis."

I stare into her face, the sincerity in her words right there for the world to see, and I can't fucking stop it. I need to connect with her. To touch her. To *claim* her.

Placing my hand back on her neck, I lean forward, pulling her face toward mine. Just as our lips are about to touch, I pause. "I'm gonna kiss you, Laynie. If you don't wa—"

She crushes her lips to mine, stopping my words before I can speak them. They're soft and sweet and taste like the strawberry wine she loves so much. My heart is hammering, and my dick swells instantly. Groaning, I pull her closer, demanding more from her sweet lips.

I never knew that kissing could be like this. The emotions that are warring for first place in my mind are overwhelming, taking a backseat only to my desire to make this woman mine. When her tongue slips in and slides smoothly across mine, I grasp her hips, pulling her over and onto me, straddling me. I can feel the heat of her pussy through the zipper on my jeans.

Her hands slide up and into my hair as she presses herself against my erection. I've never been so fucking turned on. She moans long and deep, grinding down on me slightly. Her hands slide from my hair, and before I can stop them, she slides them down the sides of my cheeks. When she reaches my scar, she stops kissing, stops grinding, and gasps in horror.

I don't even give her a fucking chance to say anything. Gently but quickly, I lift her from my lap and place her on the couch once more. Standing, I walk swiftly to the door and without a second glance, get the fuck out of there.

Tease

JUMPING ONTO MY ride, I rev the motor and peel off down the quiet street. My vision is blurred by rage. I wish more than anything that I could go back in time to the day that motherfucker cut me and rip his black heart right out of his scrawny chest. I've always prided myself on not caring what others think about my face, but when Laynie had touched my mangled cheek, I'd fucking cared. And when she'd gasped like that... *fuck!*

I knew she'd be disgusted. I'd wanted her to know who I really am – how we don't fit — but now that she knows, and I turned out to be right, I don't know what the fuck to do with it. I've gotten to know her a little. I've kissed her sweet as fuck lips and captured her moans with my tongue. *FUCK!*

This is why I never fucking put myself out there. This is why I stick to myself and don't worry about anyone else. It's been that way since he fucking ruined me. That's when I realized that everybody else was going to let me down too. The only person I could count on was myself.

After that life-changing night, I thought for sure my mother would leave him. I waited. And then I waited some more. Without

Buddy there, I was miserable, and my face took forever to heal. He never stopped cuffing me on the side of the head every time he walked by me, and that didn't help me heal either. I needed to get away. I knew if I didn't, I was going to die in that house.

But she never left. She never even fucking acknowledged what had happened. If anything, she got worse. She started drinking more and sleeping all the time, leaving me alone with Rick. One night I was in bed sound asleep when Rick came into my room. He'd smelled strongly of booze and could hardly stand up. He'd walked to the side of my bed, undoing his belt as he moved.

I bolted upright, knowing he was going to beat me with that belt, but he didn't. He'd come to the edge of my bed directly in front of me and dropped his pants. "You're fucking mother's passed out and can't suck my dick, so guess what, you little fuck...it's your turn." I'd stared at him in horror as he'd grabbed the back of my head and tried to press my face into his fully-erect and foul-smelling cock.

That was when I lost it. Bringing up my fist, I punched that drunk fuck right in the nuts, and when his knees gave out from the pain, I ran. With nothing but the pajamas I was wearing, and the shoes I managed to grab on my way out, I ran like hell.

I didn't know what the fuck to do. I was only nine years old. For days, I lived on the streets, eating out of dumpsters and sneaking into the basement of the public library to sleep. It didn't take long for me to get caught, but when my mother came into the station, she wouldn't even look at me. I watched her through the window of the interrogation room as she cried and told the police she couldn't handle me anymore; I was a trouble maker. I'd like to think this was her way of saving me – of giving me an out.

So I went into foster care. Nobody wanted a nine-year-old delinquent in their home, so I ended up in a group home for boys. Most of the kids there were in their teens. It was like moving from one level of hell to another. Those boys took one look at my mangled face and my scrawny frame and decided that my life wasn't shit enough — they needed to make it even shittier.

Every day they teased me. They called me names, kicked me, punched me, and stole my food. I tried to tell the social workers, but they didn't believe it was that bad, and besides, their hands were tied. Where else was I going to go?

I took that shit until I was sixteen. By then I had grown a lot, and I was starting to fill out and gain more muscle. One of the kids that had been harassing me for years thought it would be funny to embarrass me in front of the hottest girl in school, and I lost it. Grabbing my pencil, I'd jammed it straight through his hand and beat the fuck out of the son-of-a-bitch until the police showed up to pull me off him.

I spent the next two years in juvie. Juvenile detention centers are not a place for kids to sort their shit. It's a lot like prison, but on a smaller scale. I never made any friends there. I kept to myself, and I fought when I had to. I quickly earned a reputation for being a guy you didn't dare fuck with, and that worked for me, so I keep that reputation and wear it like a goddamned shield to this day.

All those years and all those experiences should have taught me not to fall into the trap I fell into tonight. I don't blame Laynie, I blame myself — I'd been charmed by her. She couldn't see me to know who or what I was. I was the ass that kissed her as if I had some right to claim her. For the first time, I'd forgotten who I was...*what* I was. I won't let that ever happen again.

Laynie

My face heats as I hear the door to the apartment close softly. He left. We were having an incredible time, and he left. I can't believe I had gasped like that. It must have sounded pretty awful for him to leave without a word. I'm so angry at myself.

Tears fill my eyes as I sit, waiting for him to come back. It's not until I hear the roar of his motorcycle as he speeds away that they fall onto my cheeks. *What have I done?* I knew he was broken somehow, but I didn't know how or why. I still don't, really, but I know it has something to do with that long scar I felt on his cheek.

God. What had happened to him to cause that? It wasn't overly thick or rough feeling, but I could feel its length and that it was smooth with age. That was an old scar.

I need to apologize. To let him know that I didn't mean to gasp. I'd gasped because from that single touch of his face, I knew he'd lived a hard life – that he'd been through something tragic. Something that changed his life forever. Just like me.

Picking up my phone, I direct it to call Travis. It rings seven times before I remember he's driving. Pacing back and forth, I ignore the burn in my foot from where I'd stepped on the glass. My anxiety takes over, numbing any pain. I will never forgive myself if I can't apologize to him.

Unable to take it anymore, I try his number again. I wait ten full rings before I hang up. When he checks his phone next, he's going to think I'm a stalker. I send him a text.

Laynie: Travis, I need to talk to you. Please answer your phone.

Thinking back to just a little while ago, I remember the feeling of Travis beneath me. Of his hard body firm under mine. Of his soft lips moving in rhythm with my own. Nobody had ever kissed me that way. Nobody had ever set me on fire like that. Nobody had ever even tried.

Three more times I try Travis's number, each time letting it ring a little longer and a little longer still, but he never answers. My head aches right along with my heart, and I decide it's time for me to go to bed. I will get ahold of Travis first thing in the morning and apologize, making this all better. He'll come back. He *has* to.

I take Dex out for his nightly pee and ready myself for bed, trying Travis just one last time. Still no answer. Settling under the blankets, my heart sings when my phone rings, breaking the gloomy silence in the room. I scramble for the phone, pushing the button for the verbal caller ID. It's my mother. Groaning, I bury my face in the pillow and try to get some sleep.

Tease

NO MATTER HOW fast or how far I rode last night, I couldn't get the memory of her fucking gasp from my head. I can't stop thinking about that kiss, still feeling the ghost of her lips on mine. I've reasoned with myself all day that it meant nothing — that she meant nothing — but I know I'm fucking lying.

Sitting in the back corner of the clubhouse, I drain my fourth beer of the night. I'm determined to drink until the memory fades, giving my aching heart a fucking rest. The place is packed. Whores dance around the room, tits hanging out of their shirts. Old ladies sit together in the corner, drinking and laughing. The rest of the Kings are scattered throughout the crowd, partying it up and having a great time. I wish I knew what it was like to be like them. To let loose – have fun.

A commotion by the front door drowns out the laughter around me. "Well hell-o, Barbie!" Fucking Jase. The guy is always the life of the party – never fucking serious, and tonight, I just don't want to listen to it. "Come on in, sweetheart! We don't bite!"

"Speak for yourself," someone calls out.

"Well damn. I must be at the wrong party then because I was

promised there'd be biting." My whole body freezes. *That voice.* I'm out of my seat and at the front door before Jase even gets a chance to respond. He has that flirty grin of his on his face and is reaching for her hand when I push myself between them.

Grabbing her arm, I pull her and her dog away from him and speak harshly into her ear. "How the hell did you get in here?"

She flinches, a wounded look flashing on her face before she wipes it clear of emotion. "The guy outside let me in. I told him I was with you."

Fucking Mouse. "I'll talk to him later. You need to fuckin' leave."

Another flinch. "OK. I'll leave. But first, I wanted to apologize. That kiss …" She smiles softly, and at the mention of our kiss, my heart beats a little faster. "Travis, that kiss was beautiful. I didn't–"

"Hi!" Fuck me. Both of our heads whip in the direction of the high-pitched squeal. Charlotte stands beside us, grinning from ear to ear, her cheeks rosy and flushed. She's fucking wasted. "I'm Charlotte! And you are?"

"Laynie." Laynie smiles, holding out her hand, which Charlotte captures in her own, pumping it up and down like she's trying to get fucking water out of her, a big goofy grin on her face.

"She was just leavin'." I growl out the words causing both women to look toward me and frown.

Laynie cocks a thumb in my direction. "He's mad at me."

Charlotte smirks. "He's mad at everyone."

"Yeah. Well, he's really mad at me."

Charlotte frowns. "What did you do?"

What the fuck? The two of them are standing there talking like they're at a goddamned tea social, pretending I'm not even there. I lean forward, grabbing Laynie once again. "I said she was just fuckin' leavin'."

Surprise registers on Charlotte's face just as Ryker steps up to her. "Baby girl, it looks like these two were having a conversation. Come on." Thank fuck for Ryker.

Charlotte pouts and turns back to Laynie. "It was nice to meet you, Laynie."

She smiles back. "You too, Charlotte."

Ryker wraps his arm around his woman and practically drags her back to the far side of the room. She keeps turning and waving at Laynie, a huge smile on her face, not realizing she can't see her. Looking away from her, I see almost everybody in the room is fucking watching us. My skin crawls and my gut churns when I realize that we're the center of attention at this moment. I need to get her the fuck out of here. *Now.*

Turning back to Laynie, I take one last look at the most beautiful woman I've ever seen right before I tell her to get the fuck out. It's all just too much damned drama, and I just want it to be over. "You've gotta go."

She sputters and protests as I pull her back over to the door. Jase sees us leaving and calls out to her. "Leavin' so soon, sweetheart?"

Her cheeks flame, but if her eyes could shoot sparks, they would. She's pissed. "Apparently. Travis tells me I have to leave."

Jase laughs a deep belly laugh. "*Travis* does, does he? Well, you tell Travis you want to hang out with me, and he can't make you leave." He winks at her, another person oblivious to her blindness. Anger coils in my belly at his blatant flirting.

I look at him and snarl, "Enough. Now *move*. She's leaving."

Laynie growls in anger and spins around beside me. "You know what, Travis? You seem to be the only person that has a problem with me being here. I came here to fucking apologize, and you won't even listen! I gasped, Travis. Big fucking deal. I'm sorry if I hurt your feelings, but suddenly, I don't even care if you forgive me. You really *are* a dick."

Spinning on her heel, she turns and storms out of the building, hot on Dex's tail. Jase raises his eyebrows and lets out a low whistle. "Jesus Christ, Tease. That bitch was hot! How come everyone else around here is finding hot pussy? Not cool, brother. Not cool at all." He walks away, shaking his head as if disappointed. *Ass.*

My eyes drift back to the door Laynie just walked out of, doubt starting to flood my mind. She was right. She fucking came down here, late at night, with only her dog to guide her and walked into a den of fucking bikers to apologize to me – and I may as well of spit in her face. She obviously felt bad. The least I could have done was given her a chance to clear her conscience. *Fuck. I am a dick.*

Laynie

I storm out of the clubhouse, angrier than I've ever been in my entire life. It's hard to storm anywhere when you're blind and your dog walks like a wounded turtle, but I made it work. Reaching into my purse, I pull out my phone and call the taxi company to send me another ride. Unsure of my surroundings, I lean back against the brick wall and wait.

"Uh oh." My head whips up. It's the guy who let me in. "Doesn't look like that went so well."

I grit my teeth. "It didn't. That man is impossible. He's also an asshole."

The man laughs softly before placing a cold bottle in my hand. "Beer. It's not opened yet. I wanted you to know it was safe." I smile as I take it, tears threatening to fall. "He *is* impossible. And he *is* an asshole." Damn right! "But he's also a good guy."

I scowl at him, earning myself another laugh. The truth is, I *know* he's a good guy. It was the good guy part of him that helped me when Dex got hurt and helped me again when I got drunk and cut my foot. It was the good guy part of him that slept on my couch and made me breakfast. But all those good guy actions don't mean he's a totally nice guy. "More like an asshole with good guy tendencies."

The man laughs long and hard, obviously enjoying my pain. "I like you. The name's Mouse." I wrinkle my nose at that, wondering why he has such a stupid name. I know his real name isn't Mouse, but why would he introduce himself that way? Shaking my head, I accept that I'll probably never figure it out.

Sticking out my hand, I wait for him to take it. He grasps it gently, giving it a single pump before letting go. "Laynie."

"Laynie. Pretty name." I just smile. "Like I was saying, Tease is a good guy. I should know. We're buddies. He would never admit that, but we are. That guy has had my back every single fucking time

I needed it and never once complained. I wouldn't be here if it weren't for him." He chuckles softly. "I get myself in a lot of… *situations.*"

I smile. I like this Mouse character. He seems so genuine and somewhat innocent compared to the other guys. I can tell he looks up to Travis. I just hope that Travis appreciates the friend he has in him.

"Well, Mouse, he may be there for you, but he's pretty much always a dick to me, and I'm not taking that shit from him. He's acting like a child."

"I don't blame you there." He sighs, and I hear Dexter's collar jingle as Mouse pets him. "Tease has had a shit life." I freeze, waiting for him to continue. "I don't know much about it…anything, really. But I do know it was shit. He don't talk much, and he mostly keeps to himself. I think it's hard for him to be around people. I also think you just need to be patient with him."

Deep down I know he's right. I thought the same thing myself last night before everything went all to hell. At the same time, though, that's a lot of effort to put into someone that can't seem to stand to be around you.

Just as I open my mouth to answer, the front door bangs open and then closed again, and I hear footsteps approaching us on the gravel parking lot.

"Beat it, Mouse." *Travis.*

Mouse's voice is amused when he replies, "See ya, Laynie."

Shaking my head at Travis's rudeness, I lift my hand and wave. "See ya, Mouse. And thanks for the beer."

I hear him start to say something, but it's cut off by a grunt from Travis, and then I hear his footsteps as he walks away.

I glare in the direction I think he is. "Don't worry. I'm just waiting for my taxi, and I'll be gone."

He sighs. "Laynie – I…can we just talk for a minute?" He sounds defeated.

Turning to face him, I just nod, waiting to see if the hope I am suddenly feeling is going to come back and bite me in the ass.

Tease

I HAVE NO clue what to say to her. I asked her if we could talk and now she's waiting for me to fucking say something – anything – and all I can do is stare at her sad green eyes, pissed that I was the one to make them sad in the first fucking place.

Taking a deep breath, I go for it. "I'm sorry." Her head tilts to the side, but she stays silent. She's not going to make this easy on me. Blowing out a breath, I stab my fingers roughly through my hair.

She continues to stand there, eyes pointed slightly to the left of me, face blank. I sigh heavily. "I was pissed. I'm a fuckin' monster, Laynie, and when you touched my face, you *knew*. You fuckin' *knew*." I watch as her brow creases with confusion, but she still says nothing. "You and me, we don't fit. You're fuckin' gorgeous, and I..." *Fuck.*

She stands up straighter. "You what?"

Fuck. I hate this. I don't talk about this shit. I don't talk about anything. Anger and frustration pump through my veins, my fists clenching tightly. "That fucking scar you felt? It's fucked up my whole face." I'm yelling at her, but I can't help it. I don't want to tell her this, but she has to know. "It's disgusting."

She nods. "I felt that." I look away, suddenly ashamed and not sure if I want to hear what she says next. "And I don't care if it's ugly or not. I gasped because I was surprised. Not to mention, devastated for you." I narrow my eyes and open my mouth to tell her to go fuck herself. That I don't need her fucking pity, but she cuts me off. "That scar is old. It's smooth and barely noticeable to the touch, but I can tell it's an old scar. Which tells *me* you got it when you were young."

Surprised, I watch her face, looking for any sign of her emotions. Skeptical, I sneer at her. "You got all that from touching my fuckin' face?"

She smiles slightly and nods. "When you lose your sight, you become pretty accustomed to using your other senses." She reaches out, hand searching for my face. I grab her wrist, holding it tightly between us, but she presses on. "How did you get that scar, Travis?"

My anger starts to fade, and my heart pounds an unsteady rhythm in my chest. I can't fucking tell her this. *Can I?* I've never told anyone about my fucked-up past. I stare into her eyes, seeing them filled with compassion and sincerity, and I start to crumble. Those eyes may not work the way they're supposed to, but fuck me, I can see every one of her emotions when I look into them.

Swallowing hard, I guide her hand slowly and gently place it against my stubbled cheek. Wariness causes my guts to roll. She smiles softly, and her thumb moves, gently running up and down the long scar that has ruined my life. Emotions wage war inside me. I want to recoil, rip her hand away from my face, and scream at her for making me feel these things. At the same time, the tenderness of her caress makes my defenses slowly dissolve.

"This scar doesn't define you, Travis," she whispers

Fuck. I avert my eyes, unable to look at her for a moment, trying to gather my feelings and speak a coherent fucking sentence. "*I know that. But not everyone does.*" She purses her lips, not happy with my response. "My whole fuckin' life has been one huge fight."

Tears swim in her eyes, threatening to slip over the edge. "My step-father gave me this fuckin' scar. My mother fuckin' watched him do it. That same night, he killed my fuckin' dog. The son-of-a-bitch ruined my life in a drunken rage, and my mother stayed. She *stayed*, Laynie. I kept waiting for her to leave him, but she didn't. So I ran."

A single tear slips down her cheek, but her voice is even when she whispers, "How old were you?"

"Nine," I grind the word out, not wanting her pity, but suddenly desperate for her understanding. I want her to know why I've become who I am.

Her hand slides from my cheek and down my shoulder and arm until she reaches my hand. "Did they find you?"

Staring at our linked hands, I scoff. "They never looked." I take a deep breath and force myself to continue. I need to tell her the rest so she'll finally fucking understand.

"I lived on the streets for a few days before the fuckin' cops found me. They tracked down my mom, and she told them she couldn't handle me anymore. Fuckers had me put into foster care, who then sent me to live in a goddamned group home. The little bastards that lived there beat the shit out of me every fuckin' day. I was just a scrawny kid with a fucked-up face. Easiest fuckin' target they ever had. When I was sixteen, I finally snapped and beat the shit out of one of *them*. I spent the next two years in juvie."

She smiles sadly. "Wow."

"So, I know this scar doesn't fuckin' define me, but it *has* defined how people treat me. I've had to keep to myself out of fuckin' necessity. People never fail to fuck me over."

She tilts her head to the side a little. "What about the Kings?"

I straighten my shoulders and shake my head. "The club's different. They don't give a fuck how I look. I'm one of 'em."

"Then I'm glad you've found them, Travis." She takes a step closer to me, pressing my back into the wall. "You know, I don't give a fuck how you look either." She smirks. "I can't even see you."

Her words cause a slow grin to grow on my face. How can this feisty little woman make me feel better about myself with just one short conversation? Shaking my head, I chuckle softly. "Smartass."

A warm smile spreads across her face, and I swear I feel some of the ice around my heart start to melt. "Now what?" she asks.

I stare at her, unsure of what to say. *Can I do this? Can I be with this woman, like Ryk is with Charlotte?* They make it work and seem so happy together. I never imagined I could ever have the same, but suddenly I want it. I want it so fucking bad. I reach out, take her by the hips and pull her into me, her body pressing up against mine. "I don't know."

"Well, I do."

Surprised, I look down at her.

"We need to take it slow. From the sounds of things, you have a hard time trusting people, but the truth is, Travis, I like you. A *lot*." She blushes. "I don't want to mess this up."

My heart pounds. "What do you suggest?"

"How about we start with…" She grins wickedly. "A bike ride."

A grin slowly takes over my face. "That I *can* do."

Laynie

After leaving Dex with a very happy Mouse, Travis silently leads me toward his bike. Excitement pulses through my body like an electric current. I've never been on a motorcycle before, but the thought of it has my head spinning.

Travis comes to a stop, and I stand still, silently waiting. I hear him fiddling with something before he places a heavy object on my head. I reach up and feel the hard outer shell of the helmet as he sets about doing up the chin strap.

"Ready?"

I just grin and nod before his massive hands encircle my waist, and he places me on the seat of the bike. Feeling him settle in between my legs, my excitement suddenly changes to something quite different. He's so big compared to me, his body broad and hard as a rock. Heat builds low in my belly when he fires up the bike. It grows hotter still when he reaches back and yanks me tight against him.

"Hang on." *God.* I love the sound of his growl.

And then, slowly, we're moving. I know we've hit the open road when the bike starts moving faster. I'm flying. The wind beats against my face, whipping the ends of my hair around. I laugh, pure joy filling my heart.

"This is amazing!" I holler, hoping he can hear me over the rush of the wind and the loud growl of the motor.

He reaches down, squeezing my knee briefly before speeding up even faster. I squeal in delight, holding onto him tightly with my thighs as I throw my arms up in the air and just feel it. Freedom. Absolute, uninhibited freedom.

Eventually, I lower my arms and wrap them back around Travis's waist, a grin spread from ear to ear. Ducking my head behind his back to block the wind, I do what I've wanted to do since that first time I bumped into him in the coffee shop. I count his abs.

His body stiffens as I let my fingers roam across his belly, but I don't care. I feel invincible. My breathing grows heavier as I count. There are eight in total. *Eight!* I've never touched a man's abs before, but even I know that an eight-pack is not the norm. Travis is stacked.

Feeling the bike slow, I wonder silently where we are as Travis pulls the bike down a bumpy road. Turning it off, he sits there, the only movement is that of his heavy breaths.

"Travis?"

Suddenly, I'm alone on the bike and before I even get a chance to wonder where the hell he went, his hands grasp each side of my helmet, and he slams his mouth down onto mine. I gasp in surprise before reaching up, wrapping my arms around his neck and yanking him closer.

I've kissed Travis before, but this is hotter, more passionate – claiming. He growls and grabs me by the hips, sliding my body down the seat until I'm lying flat. A moan escapes me as I run my hand down his back and cup the most magnificent ass ever made. We kiss like we need each other to breathe, hearts pounding, tongues dueling, and I don't know about his, but my head is swimming.

I want more — so much more — but I don't want to push him. I'd told him we needed to take it slow, so even though I may be ready to rip off his clothes and ride him into oblivion, I need to wait for him to take the lead. When his hand cups my breast, I am instantly aware of the sudden state of my panties. I mew into his mouth, gyrating my hips in need.

His thumb grazes over my nipple and the pleasure is so great, I gasp loudly, pulling my mouth from his to catch my breath. His body goes still, and then I feel him start to pull away, but I catch his bottom lip in my teeth and flick it with my tongue. And then I'm alone on the bike, panting and aroused, but Travis is panting from somewhere to my right.

I feel the loss in both my heart and in my clit. I want him back. "Travis?"

"I never kissed a woman before you." His breaths are heavy, but his words are growled.

"Never?" *I thought bikers were a bunch of sluts?* He doesn't respond. The thought of being his first kiss is thrilling — empowering. I've never kissed a man either. Teenage boys from my youth don't count. They aren't even in the same league as Travis.

I grin widely. "That's awesome!"

"What?" He doesn't sound like he believes me.

"That's awesome. We've kissed twice, and both times, I was amazing! You're a lucky guy."

Silence, then, "Jesus."

I giggle. After a minute, I grow serious. "Why haven't you ever kissed a woman?"

"Who the fuck would want to kiss me?" he snarls.

I don't let it bother me. Travis is harsh, but his anger isn't directed at me. "I would. Do it again. I'll prove it."

He snorts. "You're crazy."

I smile again. "I know."

His hand grasps mine, and he pulls me into a sitting position. Readjusting the helmet on my head, I move to the back of the seat. Just as he's climbing back on the bike, I call out. "Travis?"

He pauses but says nothing.

"Next time you kiss me like that, can you at least take the helmet off? Helmets aren't even a little bit sexy."

"You are the sexiest fucking thing I've ever seen," he growls before starting up the motorcycle and driving back toward the road. My heart soars. *He thinks I'm sexy!* Well…I am. The man knows what he likes. I am a crazy, sexy bitch, and he loves every second of it.

Snuggling into his back, I relax and just enjoy our ride home. We're riding in silence, my arms around him, his thumb rubbing back and forth across my knee when the roar of another engine grows louder in my ears. I hear it before I feel it. The impact from the left sends me flying. I barely register the crunch of metal as my shoulder skids across the pavement, burning my skin.

Like a bad dream, I keep sliding, hearing the bike rolling through the ditch behind me. I come to a stop and lie there, panting. Laughter and the squeal of tires rings through the haze. My skin burns, and I know I'm hurt. My right shoulder is screaming in pain, and I can't catch my breath.

"Travis?" I can barely get the words out. My chest is heaving trying to take in some air, but I can't make a sound. I lie there for a few seconds before trying again. "Travis?"

No response. Gingerly, I get up from the ground and crouch, left hand in front of me, searching for him. I call out his name a few more times, but all I hear is the pinging of hot metal and the wheezing coming from my own lungs.

Fear for Travis wells up inside me, bringing me to my knees. *What if he's dead?* It's just like Garrett. We had been in that car for hours after our accident, and the whole time he'd been dead. I couldn't have saved him because I had a head injury of my own, but I can save Travis. *I have to.*

Reaching into my back pocket, I feel the edge of my phone and slide it out. I can feel the cracks on the screen and pray that it works. Holding down the button, I hear the little ding that lets me know it's ready for me to talk, and I holler out, "Call 911!"

Tease

"I JUST HOPE he remembers what the fuck happened."

"Do you really think it was them?"

"I fucking *know* it was."

The hushed conversation is the first thing I hear as the fog lifts. Next is the constant beeping from a nearby machine. *What the fuck?* I try to open my eyes, but they feel glued shut.

"Look at her fuckin' face, man. Tease is gonna be pissed."

This last sentence, followed by a grunt of agreement, has me struggling to wake up. *Who are they talking about? Laynie? Fuck. Why can't I open my fucking eyes?* With a groan, I manage to use every fucking muscle in my face to finally get my eyelids to crack open a bit.

Through my blurred vision, I see a person move to stand over me. "Tease? Man, you OK?" Fucking Mouse.

I groan again, forcing my eyelids open farther. "Ryk! He's awake." Even though he's whispering, his voice rings loudly through my pounding head. I see Ryker step up beside him. *What the fuck is going on?*

"Hey, brother. It's fuckin' good to see you. You had us worried there for a bit."

I stare at Ryker, wondering what the fuck he's talking about when a flashback hits me. Driving with Laynie, her arms flung back in fuckin' joy, kissing her. And then, a large van coming out of nowhere and ramming into the side of us. I grit my teeth through the pain and bolt upright in bed. "Laynie?"

"Shhh. She's fine. Sleepin' in the corner so shut up, would ya?" I glare at Ryker, and he smirks. "Do you remember what happened?"

Lying back on the bed, I sigh. "Didn't see much. Fuckin' van came out of nowhere and rammed into the side of us. That's it."

"Laynie said she heard men laughing after the crash and tires squealing as they took off. It had to have been the fucking Devils."

Rage erupts in my chest, burning through me like a wildfire. I look over to where Laynie sleeps, curled up in a straight-back chair, sound asleep with Dexter at her feet. She has scrapes covering half of her face, on her cheek, and chin. The rage builds. Those fuckers almost killed us – almost killed her. They are going to die, and *I'm* the one that's going to make it happen.

"She's fine, man." I spear Ryker with my eyes. *Fine?* She's covered in road rash. "She's pretty scraped up, but mostly she's been worried about you. You had a head injury that made it a little scary there for a while. She'll be glad you're awake."

I stare at her again, pissed that she got caught up in our club shit. "They're gonna die."

"They are. We're gonna fuckin' kill every last one of those cocksuckers," Ryker growls.

I look down at the wires and tubes sticking out of me and clench my jaw. "Let's go."

Ryker chuckles. "Not happenin', man. You're gonna be here a while yet. Sit back and get better. We won't move on the sons-of-bitches until you get out." I glare at him, jaw clenched. The need to draw blood from the Devils nearly undoes me. I need to get out of here.

Just then, the doctor walks in. He opens his mouth to say something, but I cut him off. "Take these fuckin' tubes out of me. I'm leavin'."

His eyebrows raise in surprise, but he just looks down at his clip-board. "Mr. Hale. You suffered trauma to the head and severe skin abrasions to twenty percent of your body. You were unconscious for more than twelve hours. You won't be going anywhere."

"Fuck yo —"

"Travis?" Her sleep clouded voice calls out in distress from the other side of the room and all of our heads turn toward her.

"I'm here, babe."

Tears fill her eyes, and she sits upright, gathering the blanket from her lap as she stands. "Oh, honey. I was so scared." She reach-es out, hands searching for the bed as she walks toward me. I move my arm to meet her, but pain slices through me when I do.

"That would be the abrasions," the doctor whispers.

I narrow my eyes at him just as Laynie reaches the bed. Tears are freely flowing down her cheeks. My gut tightens. I hate seeing her like this. Our hands finally meet, and she grasps mine tightly in hers. "Are you OK?"

"Will be as soon as this fuckin' doctor lets me go the hell home," I growl, eyes narrowed on the dick in the lab coat.

"Go home?" A crease forms between her brows. "You can't go *home*! You were hurt in a motorcycle accident, Travis."

No shit. "And now I'm fuckin' fine."

"You're not! You had a head trauma. They aren't something to take lightly. Take it from me."

How the fuck can I argue with that? Gritting my teeth, I flop my head back onto the pillow. Ryker chuckles, and Mouse makes a whip cracking sound with his mouth. I whip my head to glare at them, try-ing to pierce them with my eyes as the doctor starts listing off my medical concerns.

I don't give a fuck. I just want to get out of here and kill those bastards. They almost killed Laynie. The doctor's still talking when I cut off his speech. "How long?"

He looks me directly in the eyes. I have to give the man respect. He doesn't seem to be afraid of me at all. "We need to keep you un-der observation for at least twenty-four hours."

"Fuck."

Ryker clears his throat. "All right. I'm gone. Rest up, brother. This is just the beginnin'."

Defeated, I just nod. Mouse turns to Laynie. "You need a ride?"

"No. I'm going to stay here with Travis and make sure he stays in that bed." I scowl at her.

Mouse laughs. "Gotcha. See ya, Tease." He leans in and kisses Laynie on the cheek. I want to rip the fucker's lips off. "See ya, gorgeous."

"Bye, Mouse. Bye, Ryker," she calls.

They leave the room, and I turn to face Laynie. She smiles and runs her hand across the bed. Determining there's enough room for her, she climbs up and curls next to me with her head on my shoulder. Needing to keep her close, I pull the blankets up over her and wrap my uninjured arm around her waist.

Kissing my pec, she mumbles, "I'm so glad you're OK."

I give her a squeeze and feel the pull of sleep dragging me down. I bury my nose into her strawberry-smelling hair, and after only a few seconds, I fall fast asleep.

Laynie

I wake up draped across Travis's chest. I nuzzle him with my cheek thinking he's still asleep when I notice that he's lying beneath me, stiff as a board. I sit up quickly, worried that I'm hurting him somehow.

"Travis?"

Silence, then, "You need to go."

I jerk in surprise, frowning deeply. "What?"

"You heard me." He sounds angry, and I don't understand what's going on.

I place my uninjured hand on his cheek. "Why?"

"We can't do this. It's not safe."

Confused, I pull back, wishing more than anything I could see his face. "What's not safe?"

"This. Us. We can't do it. Shit's goin' on with the club, and it's only gonna get worse."

Confusion gives way to anger. Swinging my legs over the side of the bed, I stand. "That's bullshit, and you know it."

"You almost fucking *died*!" he roars.

I step closer, leaning over the bed, and calmly say, "But I didn't." He says nothing. And then it dawns on me. "You're scared."

He scoffs. "Of what?"

I throw my hands up in the air. "Of us."

"Fuck that." I can hear the venom in his voice, but I don't let it faze me. I'm tired of his back and forth bullshit.

"You are. You're using the first excuse that comes along to end this between us before it even gets started. You're scared, and you're pushing me away." Silence. "For fuck's sake, Travis, it's not like I'm asking you to fucking marry me! I *like* you. I want to get to know you. I —"

"Why?"

Surprised by the question, I cock my head slightly. "Why what?"

"Why the fuck do you want to get to know me so bad?" Sarcasm laces his tone.

The man is clueless. "Well...you're pretty ripped." I smirk. "And kind...sometimes, anyways. I like your gruff voice and your chuckle. You smell amazing. But most of all...you treat me like a normal person." I shrug and cast my eyes downward, biting my lip. "You actually listen to me. Sometimes I don't even remember that I'm blind when I'm with you."

He groans like he's in pain. "Fuck."

I can't do this anymore. I won't. I'm tired and sore, and I need a shower. Travis pushing me away after the nightmare I lived of trying to find him after the accident has drained what's left of my patience and my energy. I snap my fingers to call Dex over, and once he reaches my side, I grab his harness and say what I need to say.

"You want me to leave, I'll leave. Not forever...just for now. But you have some major soul searching to do, Travis. My emotions can't be played with like a goddamned yo-yo. Stop masking those massive fears you have with your tough guy act, and maybe, hopefully, you'll finally be happy. I just really hope I'm the one you choose to be happy with." I take a deep breath and finish. "So this is not goodbye…more of a see you soon. We never got to finish that ride." Tossing a tired smile over my shoulder, I turn and walk out of the room.

I know he doesn't mean for me to hear it when he mutters, "Fuckin' nut."

Tease

THE NEXT MORNING, Ryker and Mouse are there to spring me when the doctor finally gets off his ass and gives the all clear to escape the creepy hospital room. Ryker gives me a fresh set of clothes, and after I finish getting dressed, we pile into the black, un-marked van the club uses when they need to keep a low profile.

"Your bike is fucked, brother." I knew it would be, but hearing it confirmed just about fucking kills me. I love that bike. "Jase says he can fix it. He was working on it when we left."

I clench my jaw and nod. I know Jase can fix it – the man is a fucking genius with motorcycles. I just don't look forward to not having my ride until he does. Looks like I'll be driving this fucking van for a while.

"Where's Laynie?" Ryker asks.

I side-eye him. "Gone."

"Gone? Not for good, though, right?" Mouse pokes his head up between the two front seats. "Laynie's the shit!"

I glare straight ahead, watching the scenery and thinking that Mouse needs to learn to mind his own fucking business.

"He's right, ya know." I look at Ryker. "She's fuckin' cool. And she likes you, which is a miracle in its-fucking-self. Hold on to that shit, brother."

I shake my head, noticing the driveway for the clubhouse approaching. I need to get out of this vehicle and away from these nosey fucks. Ryker just chuckles and pulls into the nearest parking space. "Church in five."

The three of us walk into the clubhouse and are greeted by Gunner. "Get your asses in the meeting room. We're all waiting. Mouse, you better sit in on this one."

Mouse nods and follows us in. Once we're all seated, Gunner pounds his gavel down onto the table. "Shit's gettin' serious, boys. Real serious." He motions to me. "Tease, glad you're OK, brother."

I receive slaps on the back and murmured agreements before he continues. "Those sons-of-bitches almost killed one of our own last night. And he had his fuckin' old lady with him." My heart clenches at the mention of Laynie. After the way her brother died, she must have been fucking terrified. Breaking it off with her was a shit move.

"They wanted a war? Well, they fuckin' got one." Fists pound the table, and the room erupts in loud voices, each one plotting the death of the Devil's Rejects. All except one.

"How do we even know it was the Devils?" The room quiets, and all eyes turn to Tiny. "We have no proof. Tease was fuckin' knocked out, and his bitch is fuckin' blind." He sneers that last word with disgust.

My eyes widen, and heated rage erupts in my gut. I pierce him with my eyes, about to lose my shit when I'm interrupted.

"You might want to watch your tone more carefully next time, Tiny," Reaper growls. "You disrespect a brother or his old lady like that again, I'll be next in line after Tease to shove my foot up your ass and wear you as a fuckin' boot."

Tiny's eyes narrow on Reaper, but he says nothing. Gunner shakes his head. "Moving on, ladies. We know it was the Devils for sure because I have a contact who fuckin' told me so."

I sit up straighter, ignoring the pain from my road rash. This is news to me.

"A man that goes by the name of Tip contacted me earlier this mornin'. He's an advisor for the local chapter of the Bloods." He looks around the room. "Seems we got a common enemy."

"The Bloods? We're doing business with the fuckin' Bloods now?" Tiny shakes his head. "Fuck me."

"Tiny!" Gunner yells his name so loud we all jump. "Shut the fuck up, or get the fuck out of my clubhouse. I'm tired of dealin' with you and your fuckin' mouth. Show some goddamned respect or hand in your fuckin' patch." Tiny's eyes widen. "Moving the fuck on. Tip has a guy workin' undercover with the Crips. Said the Crips and the Devils have been workin' together on some drug trading lately. He overheard them last night laughin' about runnin' one of the Kings off the road."

He leans back in his chair. "Now, Tip didn't give me this information out of the kindness of his heart. The Bloods want the Crips taken out. They want their share of the cocaine trade here in the city, and the Crips are seriously fuckin' with their business. There's a drop-off tonight outside of an old warehouse near the airport. The Devils are pickin' up a bunch of coke and takin' it back to Toronto. We now have the location and the time. The deal is, we take out the Devils and in the process take out a few Crips along the way."

A frown creasing his forehead, Jase sits up. "The fuck? That's just gonna cause war with the fuckin' Crips. Is that wise?"

Gunner sighs. "Probably not, but it's a perfect opportunity for a hit. They won't be expectin' us. The Bloods are good allies to keep. We do this, they'll have our backs when we need them."

"I don't like it," Ryker states, echoing my own thoughts. "Starting a war with the Crips is just jumping from one war to another."

"It's decided. We're not voting on this. As your president, this is a direct fucking order." Gunner glares at Ryker, daring him to argue.

Ryker shakes his head, clearly not happy. "So what's the plan?"

"We get there early and lay low. We wait 'til they all get there, and in the middle of their exchange, we open fire." He nods to Reaper. "Reap, you're the best shot of all of us. You're snipin'."

Reaper nods.

"These stupid fucks picked the wrong goddamned club to mess with. Runnin' our man off the road signed their death certificates."

Ryker and I lock eyes. Doing this mission may just be us signing our own.

Laynie

Travis has been out of the hospital for hours now. I know because I called, and they told me he'd been released. That was three hours ago. I'd figured after my epic monologue and dramatic exit, he'd have at least called. That's what any one of my super sexy book boy-friends would do – especially the bikers. They are all badasses, but they take care of their old ladies. Too bad they're all fictional. *Is that what I am now? His old lady?* I don't know if we'd gotten that far yet.

I'm thankful that he's out of the hospital, though. It means that he's OK. I'd thought I had lost him. From the moment I'd heard that car peel away, tires squealing on the asphalt, I'd searched for him. I must have looked like a lunatic when the paramedics showed up. I was crying hysterically, on my hands and knees, searching with both hands patting the air, trying to find him. He wouldn't answer me no matter how much I'd screamed his name. The nightmare I'd suffered the night I lost my vision, and my brother had returned. I was in the middle of nowhere, hurt and afraid, and utterly helpless.

Maybe walking away from that hospital room yesterday had been a mistake, but I stand by my decision. Travis doesn't handle his emotions well, and although I'd gotten angry, I know that he was only pushing me away because he didn't know what else to do. I won't let him get away that easily. Travis deserves to be loved. He just doesn't know it yet.

I've done what I can to keep busy since I got home yesterday. My apartment is spotless. I've listened to the last of my books I was to read this week. I wrote and scheduled my blog posts for the up-coming week. I paid my bills and walked my dog. I even baked my world famous, double chocolate chunk cookies, which I usually only make when Daniel begs me to. I'd also avoided my hysterical moth-er.

The woman has called non-stop, but I just can't deal with her right now. I have my own issues to deal with, and none of them involve playing the role of her poor, defenseless, little blind girl. If Mom found out about my accident, she would drive me crazy begging me to come back home. I'd never do it, though. I love my independence. I love the city. Most of all, I love the freedom.

Deciding that Travis isn't coming tonight after all, I change into my pajamas – a tiny little silk tank with matching booty shorts. I'm just crawling into bed when my phone rings again. It's my mother. *Why? Why can't she just leave me the hell alone?*

Pulling the blankets up over my head, I think about Travis and wonder if I'm going to have to track him down. Did he mean what he said when he told me we couldn't do this? Did my speech about him being afraid make him crawl even further into his shell? Thinking about the way he held me all night makes my eyes fill with tears. I know he feels something for me; I just hope he doesn't forget that while he's trying to sort his head out.

Tease

WE'VE BEEN CROUCHING on top of these abandoned shipping containers for two hours now. The containers are perfect for this. Ten of them surround the parking area of the abandoned warehouse. My body is killing me, and I'm beginning to wonder if this was just a distraction when the motorcycles pull into the parking lot. There are six of them.

It's not all of the Devils, but every one of them is a patched member, and every one of them is going to die tonight. Adrenaline causes the blood to pound through my aching head while we wait for the Crips to show up. I don't like this plan. Starting a war with the Crips is not a smart move, but we don't really have a fucking choice in the matter.

Shortly after, a big black Cadillac drives in, entering the circle of shipping containers. We watch as five men climb from the car. Each one wears a blue shirt and baggy jeans. The Crips have arrived. Ryker looks to Reap and nods. Gritting his teeth, Reaper puts his eye back to the scope and makes some small changes to his position. The silencer on the gun makes the shot quieter, and the men on the ground don't even get a chance to respond before one of the members of the Devils is on the ground, blood pouring from a hole in his head.

After that, everything happens in a blur. As one, each man whips out their guns, ducking and scanning the area for shooters, but we have them surrounded. Taking aim, I fire my shots, praying that I get the son-of-a-bitch that drove into the side of my ride. Gunshots ring through the air followed by shouts and curses as one by one we take out each man on the ground.

They shoot back wildly, unable to get a clear shot. Each shot they do take goes right through the shipping container, riddling it with holes. When the last man is on the ground, I look to each container, ensuring that my brothers are OK. There are only nine of us standing on our containers, looking down into the carnage below.

"Reap! I need a fuckin' medic!" Jase hollers.

Reaper rushes down the side of his container, hurrying toward Jase. "What happened?" he yells as he runs across the lot.

"The fuckers shot me!"

Each of us turns and hurry to the ground focused on Jase, so it takes us all by complete surprise when one of the Crips jumps up and runs to the car he'd arrived in. We all raise our guns, firing shots wildly at the departing car as it peels out of the parking lot and fishtails down the street.

"Fuck!" Ryker yells. "Fuck! Fuck! Fuck!"

That guy getting away is not fucking good. He saw us. Now the Crips are going to know exactly who ambushed their fucking coke deal, and they aren't going to like it. Remembering Jase, we all turn to where Reaper already has him sitting on the ground against the container, looking him over.

"You fuckin' pussy," he growls. "They didn't fuckin' shoot you. They *grazed* you."

"Grazed my fuckin' ear! My ear! I can't have a fucked up ear! Ladies don't want some dumb fuck with a fucked-up ear!" Jase cries. "Fuckin' fix it!"

"For fuck's sake." Reaper stalks off toward the bikes. "Get your ass back to the clubhouse and I'll put a damned Band-Aid on it."

Shaking my head, I turn and head for the van, glad that I'm not a fucking prospect anymore. Mouse and our newest prospect have their work cut out for them. There are ten bodies here that need to be disposed of, and it needs to be done fast. The Crips will be back, and soon.

I have my own mess to clean up. I need to go to Laynie and apologize.

Laynie

The pounding on the door yanks me from my sleep. *Who the hell is at my door in the middle of the night?* Throwing back the covers, I run my hands along the wall and hurry to get it before it wakes up the entire neighborhood.

Pressing my face close to it, I call out, "Hello?"

From the other side of the door, I hear, "It's Travis."

Hurrying to unlock the deadbolt, I call out, "How'd you get in here?"

I swing the door open, and his voice is clearer when he answers "The douche across the hall let me in."

"Oh." I don't know what else to say. Awkwardness fills the space between us.

"Hi."

He sounds so unsure. I can't help but smile. "Hi," I say softly.

More silence. I can hear the creak of leather and the whisper of his hair as he runs his fingers through it. "So?" I put my hand on my hip, leaning against the open door. "What can I do for you, Travis?"

I know that him showing up here is his way of apologizing, and I know that words aren't easy to express for him, but he hurt me – again. He needs to know that he can talk to me, but he also needs to apologize and stop pulling that crap with me.

He groans loudly. "Fuck."

Not saying a word, I wait patiently for him to say what I need him to say.

"I hate this shit." He presses his body up against mine, hands resting on my hips. "You were right."

My heart swells and a small knowing smile grows on my face. "I always am."

He chuckles as he puts a hand to my belly, guiding me backward so he can close the door. "Don't push it." Taking a seat on the couch, he pulls me down onto his lap. "You were right when you said I was pushin' you away out of fear. I knew I was gonna fuck this up with you. I fuckin' knew it. I'm sorry, Laynie." His hand wraps around the back of my head, and he pulls my face to his. "You walkin' out of that hospital yesterday fuckin' gutted me. That's not gonna happen again. You're mine, and I'm not gonna do anything else to fuck that up."

A single tear slides down my cheek as I smile, feeling his breath fan across my face. "I thought you weren't coming." Sitting up slightly, I give him a light smack on the chest. "What took you so freakin' long?"

He spins me around, my knees resting on either side of him. "I had some shit to take care of. Now that's done, and I ain't fuckin' going anywhere."

A small smile tugs at my lips, but I fight it back. "So I'm stuck with you?"

He growls and moves again, flipping me to my back and pinning me to the couch with his massive body. "You got a problem with that?"

I manage to keep a straight face and nod. "I do."

He pulls back slightly. "Tough." A giggle jumps from my throat and is cut short when he sucks in a breath. "Fuck me, babe. What've you got on?"

I blink. "Um…jammies?"

He groans. "Jesus." He puts a hand on my knee and runs it slowly up to my hip leaving a trail of fire where he touched me. "I ain't a virgin."

Biting my lip, I nod. "I know." I swallow, forcing down the lump in my throat. "I am."

"Shit." He buries his face in my neck. "You have no idea how fuckin' hot that makes me, knowin' I'll be the only one to ever be inside you." His hips grind down on mine, and I can feel his hardness pressing into me. My heart pounds in my chest. "I ain't a virgin but I never let any one of those bitches I've fucked touch me."

He grabs my hand, lifting it to his scarred cheek and pressing it tightly against his face. "I fuckin' *need* you to touch me, Laynie."

God. This man. Sliding my hand down his face, I run it down his chest and belly until I reach the waist of his jeans. Shoving my hand up and under his shirt, my fingers explore his smooth hardness, and I whisper, "I need to touch you too."

He groans, his chest rumbling beneath my fingers, just as his lips graze my own. Electricity shoots through my body, the blood rushing behind my ears as our lips slide together gently. Tasting. Sipping. Savoring one another. I'm surrounded by his delicious scent as my fingers go from touching to grasping. I need him. I need him closer. I need him *now*.

My heart aches from the sweetness of his kiss. I find it hard to believe that I'm the first woman ever to feel this man's tenderness. He has so much to offer any woman, and I feel special that it's me he chose to share that part of himself with.

Wanting to make him feel as special as I do, I run my palm back down his chest and slowly reach down, cupping him through his jeans. *Oh my God.* He is freaking huge. The heat from his hardness radiates up my arm and right down to my clit making it pulse with excitement. Growling deep in his chest, he pushes himself against my palm.

"Fuck, Laynie," he rasps.

His mouth slams down onto mine, his tongue demanding entrance. My heart soars, beating out of time. Feeling his hand on my waist, my breath catches when he rips my tank-top up and off of my body. He hisses through his teeth, and I feel his hands span my belly.

Not sure what that means, I squirm slightly before I feel his lips wrap around my nipple, sucking it in deep. Spearing my hands through his hair, I arch my back and whimper loudly. My head swims and my lungs struggle for air as he flicks his tongue across my nipple, squeezing my breast roughly in his huge, calloused hand.

He releases my breast with a loud pop, and then drags his tongue across the tight, sensitive bud. Running it across to my other breast, he stops, gently tugging on the nipple with his teeth. My eyes roll back in my head as I cry out.

His lips claim mine once more, his hips grind against me, his hard cock rubs against my clit through our clothes. I wrap my arms around him tightly, pushing my tongue into his mouth, savoring the taste of him on my tongue. I will never forget his taste for as long as I live.

He pulls away suddenly, lips trailing down my neck and breasts, and his tongue stops to swirl inside the deep crevice of my belly button. I feel his fingertips at the sides of my booty shorts just as he whisks them away.

His body settles between my legs, and I feel his rapid breaths fanning across my moist center, but he doesn't move. I whimper and rotate my hips, needing him to touch me. To lick me. To just take away this damn ache.

I don't feel vulnerable in this moment. I feel safe. I know that Travis would never do anything to hurt me, and I can tell by the raggedness of his breathing that he is just as turned on as I am. I've wanted to have this with a man for years, and I could have a few times, but it never felt right. Right here, in this moment, I am so glad I waited for *him*.

Then I feel the moist firmness of his tongue flick across my clit once. Then again. Then one more time. My heart pounds wildly, and I cry out with each flick of his tongue, not caring who hears me. He growls then, pressing his hands against my inner thighs, forcing my legs open as wide as they'll go as he buries his face into my greedy pussy.

Screaming, my hips buck as he sucks and nips and licks me into a frenzy. Using a single finger, he continues to lick me as he slides it deep inside. Words pour from my mouth, but I don't have a clue what I'm saying. I feel out of breath, out of body, and most definitely out of mind.

He places a second finger inside me and thrusts them deeply. His tongue flattens and presses hard as he sweeps it quickly over my nub. I can feel the pressure building deep in my belly and heat builds behind my clit, scorching me in the most delicious way.

With one final flick of his tongue, my muscles clamp down tight on his fingers and lights burst in my head. The orgasm tears through me, making my body tremble and loud screams to erupt from my throat. I've orgasmed before, and it was always good, but each time had been self-induced — this orgasm put every one of those to shame.

I lie there limp and panting, body still racked with tremors while Travis runs his tongue back up my body. He kisses me sweetly, the taste of myself heavy on his tongue. It drives me wild tasting myself on him.

Grabbing his shirt, I rip it over his head, licking and sucking every bit of bare flesh I can get my mouth on. I fumble awkwardly with his belt buckle, desperate to get him out of his pants. He chuckles softly and whispers in my ear, "Babe. Relax. It's not a fuckin' race."

Pulling my teeth from his nipple, I point my face in the direction of his and plead with him. "Travis. Please."

"Fuck." Just as frantically, I hear him wrestling with his pants and the crinkle of a condom wrapper before he settles back between my legs. The sensation of his cock against my belly makes my breath catch in my throat.

"Laynie." He tilts my chin and pauses. "If we do this, there ain't no fuckin' goin' back."

I nod frantically, butterflies coursing through my belly.

His thumb presses deeper into my chin. "I fuckin' mean it. We do this, you're mine. Always."

I smile softly, eyes filling with tears. "Travis, I've been yours since I slammed into you at the coffee shop. You just didn't know it yet."

He growls then, taking my mouth in a fast, hard kiss. I feel his cock at my entrance, pushing in slightly. I rotate my hips, willing him to go deeper. "This is gonna hurt," he whispers, voice heavy with regret.

I nod. "I know. Just do it. Please."

He moves his hips slowly, the tip going in and out, and it feels so fucking good. And then he drives his cock to the hilt. Pain tears through me, making me cry out and my fingernails to dig into his back. Travis doesn't move, his body trembling with the effort to stay still.

After a few moments, my body adjusts, and the pain fades. Removing my claws from his back, I rotate my hips, wanting to feel more of him. His breath comes out in a shudder as he starts to move. Slowly, he glides in and out, his cock filling me — completing me — but still I need more.

I know he's trying to be gentle, but the ache in my clit is back, and my body is on fire. Reaching up, I grab his cheeks, pulling his face to mine. "Travis! Fuck me!"

He grunts, grabbing my hips as he slams down into me. With every thrust, I push deeper and deeper into the couch. His thumb comes down on my clit, and that's exactly what I needed. My muscles clamp down on his cock, and my whole body flushes as the heat from my orgasm takes over. His thrusts become frantic and uneven just before he yells out my name in a throaty voice. "Laynie!"

Digging my fingernails into his back, I roll my hips into his, savoring the feeling of him inside me as long as I can. His body quivers with his own release, and his thrusts slow as his orgasm leaves him. Grunting in exhaustion, he flops down on top of me trying to catch his breath.

I can't breathe. The man easily outweighs me by a hundred pounds. Barely able to get the words out, I grunt, "Travis. Can't. Breathe."

He lifts his body off of mine, chuckling as he moves. "Sorry." I giggle softly, reaching up to touch his face. He leans in and presses his forehead to mine. "Do you have any idea how fuckin' gorgeous you are?"

My heart warms and my face splits wide with my smile. "No, but that's OK because I have you to remind me now."

Wrapping his arms around me, he squeezes me tightly. "Goddamned right you do."

Tease

WAKING UP THE next morning, I feel a heavy weight on my chest. Laynie is sound asleep, her naked body draped over mine. The sun streams in her windows and shines against her face. Staring at her, my heart contracts tightly in my chest. Fuck, she's beautiful. And she's mine. I'm just trying to decide on the most creative way to wake her up when a cold, wet nose buries itself in my armpit.

I jump slightly, whipping my head to the side of the bed. Dexter. He sits on the floor, staring at me with intelligent eyes, his leash neatly hanging from his mouth. A grin spreads across my face. "Gotta take a leak, buddy?" I whisper, slowly climbing from the bed, trying not to wake Laynie. I have other plans on how I want to wake her up.

Sliding into my jeans, I throw on my t-shirt and boots and head for the door. While leaving the apartment, I see douchebag from next door standing at his doorway, his key in the lock, wide eyes on me. I feint in his direction as if I'm going to hit him and roll my eyes when he screams and locks himself in his own apartment.

Fucking pussy.

Holding the leash, I follow along behind Dexter as he does his business and then head back inside. As soon as I let him off his leash, he runs to the corner and grabs his stuffed rabbit. The thing is mangy and covered in dirt, looking like a piece of rabbit roadkill. Dexter seems to love it, though. I shake my head as he mounts it and proceeds to hump it even further into the grave.

Hearing a key in the lock, I spin around and move toward the door.

Who the fuck is that? It opens wide, and a tall, muscled police officer walks into the apartment. *What the fuck?*

"Who the fuck are you?" I growl, moving to block him from coming any further.

"No. Who the fuck are *you?*" he growls back, eyes narrowed as he places his hand on the butt of his revolver.

Just then, Laynie wanders into the room, wearing nothing but a short as shit little silk robe and a smile. "Travis? Honey, you here?"

The pig at the door growls and moves toward her, but I block him, shoving him back with my hand firm on his chest.

"Laynie! What the fuck happened to your face?"

Her face pales at the sound of his voice, and my stomach drops. *What the fuck is going on?* She bites her lip, uncertainty clear on her face. "Um, well...I had a little accident."

"A little accident? You look like you've been put through a damned meat grinder! Who the fuck *is* this guy? And what the fuck are you wearing?" He shoves me back, but I stand firm, eyes pinning him to the spot. "Laynie! Goddamnit. Answer me!"

Laynie squares her shoulders and clears her throat. "Daniel, meet Travis, my..."

"Her man." I drop my hand and take a step back. She'd called him Daniel. This is her fucking brother...and he's a fucking cop. *Wonderful.*

"Her man?" He stares at me in disbelief before turning his attention back to Laynie. "Your man? Laynie? What the fuck is going on?"

"I think Travis just told you that."

"Travis? His fucking name is Travis? You can't see this fucking guy, Laynie! One look at him and I can tell he's a fucking criminal!" Even though he's right, it takes every bit of willpower I have not to drive my fist into his face. I watch Laynie, waiting for the moment when she realizes her mistake.

"I can't see him, but I *know* him, and when you're in *my* house you'll respect him." Her voice is firm and leaves no room for arguments, but I can tell she respects this man, so I stay quiet.

Daniel curses, "Jesus." He puts his hands on his hips, eyes moving from me to Laynie. "Is this why you skipped out on our weekend? Do you have any idea how worried Mom is?"

"I do. She's called me seven thousand times! I'm a grown woman, Daniel. I can make my own choices. I don't need to run to Mommy's every other fucking weekend."

"Take care of yourself? Fuck, Laynie. Look at your face! Is that how you take care of yourself?"

She closes her eyes and sighs heavily. "Daniel. I love you. Please don't make this harder than it has to be.

He glares at her, clenching his jaw and shaking his head before turning to face me. "If you fucking hurt her —"

"I won't," I say solemnly, staring him directly in the eye. "But if you know Laynie at all, you'll know that she can take care of herself."

He holds my stare, the anger fading a little from his eyes. After a few long, tense seconds, he nods. "Fair enough. But know I'll be fucking watching you."

I nod back. "Wouldn't be a good brother if you didn't."

His eyes narrow, and he looks back to Laynie. She's standing in that tiny robe, hair rumpled and sexy, biting her kiss-swollen lips. "Jesus." He shakes his head and turns back to the door. "I've gotta get to work. Call me later, Squirt."

Her face breaks out in a small smile as she nods. Closing the door firmly behind him, he leaves. At the sound of the door closing, her smile falls. "I'm so sorry, Travis."

I move toward her, wanting to put that smile back on her face. "Don't worry about it. You're lucky to have him."

She smiles a teary smile and nods. "I am." I wrap my arms loosey around her waist and drag her into me, pressing my length against her belly. Her head tips to the side. I've learned she does this when she's listening for something, so I stay quiet. "Where's Dexter?"

I chuckle. "Still in the corner, humping the fuck out of that poor defenseless rabbit.

Her eyes pop, growing wider than I've ever seen them. "What?" She snaps her fingers, causing the dog to come instantly, leaving the rabbit lying on the ground. "He was not."

I grin. "Babe. He was. He fuckin' loves that thing."

Her nose wrinkles in disgust. "He just likes to play with it!"

"The way that thing looks, I'd say he likes to fuck it. A lot."

Her face contorts. "Dexter! Ew!"

I can't contain the laugh that erupts from inside my chest. She looks so disgusted, and the fucking dog is sitting there looking at her, head cocked to the side in confusion. It's priceless.

Tears gather in my eyes as I hug her to me, shoulders shaking with laughter.

When I stop, we stand pressed against one another, the dog still staring at us. Reaching up, I wipe the tears from my eyes and smile down at her. Her face is soft and smiling. "What?"

"You have the most beautiful laugh I've ever heard," she whispers. I stare into her face, heart filling with something I'm definitely not ready for and swallow. "It's also very sexy."

Her hands run down my back, gripping my ass tightly.

"You know what else is sexy?" I say nothing as I run my hand under the veil of long hair at the nape of her neck. "The way you didn't take shit from my brother."

Using both hands to pull my ass forward, she rubs her belly against my hardening cock and bites her lip. Groaning, I claim her mouth with my own, using my teeth to tug on her lower lip.

Tearing her lips away, she whispers between heavy breaths, "I want to show you how very fucking sexy you are."

"Me first," I growl.

She squeals in delight as I grab her waist and lift her up. Wrapping her legs around my waist, I try to keep up with her kiss as I carry her off to her bedroom.

Laynie

It's been a week since Travis and I had our little heart to heart, and it has been the most amazing week of my life. During the day, he goes off and does whatever it is an outlaw biker does while I go to work in the mornings and blog or read in the afternoons. He usually shows up at my place around supper time, and we spend the rest of the night talking and exploring each other's bodies, finding new ways to pleasure one another.

Today he was home by lunch time. After ripping the headset from my ears, and setting my computer aside, Travis had thrown me over his shoulder and carried me into the bedroom. In there, he'd made my toes curl by drawing three back to back orgasms from my body. Three!

Now, it's almost three o'clock, and we're sitting on the patio of the very coffee shop we'd met at, enjoying the sounds of the people rushing up and down the street. I love it here. It's where I do my best work, but today, I'm content just to sit here, in the presence of my man, and smile at the awesomeness that is my life.

"Tease?" a voice calling his name pulls me from my thoughts.

"Fuck me," he mutters.

The voice is closer now. "Tease? Is that you?"

"Who is it?" I whisper.

"Nobody. Let's go." He grabs my arm and tries to pull me into a stand, but I frown, forcing my ass to stay in my chair.

"It is you!" The woman sounds breathless...and familiar. "I was just heading into work and thought I saw you over here. Hi, Laynie."

Confused, I frown, but answer with a, "Hi."

"It's Charlotte," she giggles.

"Oh! Hi, Charlotte! Nice to see you again!" I gesture to our table. "Please. Have a seat."

"Oh. I can't. I do have to get to work. I was just surprised to see Tease here, and well...I'm kind of nosey." I can hear the smile in her voice and decide instantly that I like this woman. "But hey, I would love to hang out with you sometime."

"That would be great." A smile crawls across my face. I haven't had a girlfriend since my accident. And never one as nice as Charlotte seems to be.

"Fuck me," Travis mutters again.

Charlotte ignores him. "I'll talk to Ryker. Him and Tease can figure something out!"

"Fuck that."

"Travis!" Honestly. Sometimes he can be the rudest man alive. "You do that, honey. I look forward to it."

"Great! I gotta go. Talk to you later, Laynie." I can hear her footsteps moving away slowly. "Bye, Tease."

"Bye, Charlotte," I call out. Travis says nothing.

I narrow my eyes in his direction and declare, "I want to go."

"Jesus."

Smiling, I finish what's left of my coffee. This is going to be fun.

Tease

I'M IN THE garage at the clubhouse with Jase and Mouse working on my bike, when Ryker walks in. One look at him, and I fuckin' know what he's here to say.

"Hear you saw Charlie yesterday." I glare at him and turn back to the bike. "She wants to go on a double date."

I whip my head in his direction. "Not fuckin' happenin'."

He grins. "She said you'd say that." Jase and Mouse stop their work and are watching the two of us like we're in a goddamned tennis match. "What's the big deal, man? Let's just take 'em out, get 'em loaded, then go home and fuck the shit out of 'em."

I hesitate, thinking that actually doesn't sound too bad. "Where?"

"We could go to the Hard Rock Café."

"Fuck no." I hate places like that.

"OK..." Ryker crosses his arms and leans against the grease-covered tool bench. "Where do *you* want to go?"

"Nowhere." I know I'm being an ass, but I don't go on fuckin' dates. And I certainly don't go on *double* fucking dates.

Jase laughs, the sound echoing throughout the large garage. "You're not gonna get this son-of-a-bitch to go anywhere."

Ryker chuckles and steps away from the bench. "Come on, Tease. It won't be so bad."

Narrowing my eyes, I turn back to the bike once more. "Why don't we all go?" Mouse asks. Grabbing a small set of pliers, I whip them in his direction. They soar past his head as he ducks, hand going up in the air. "Seriously. I can bring Sarah."

Jase chokes out a laugh. "Who the fuck is Sarah?"

Mouse straightens, shoulders square and jaw tight. "Sarah is my old lady. She's carrying my baby." He looks more serious than I've ever seen him look when he stares each one of us in the eye. "I'm going to ask her to marry me."

Jase's eyebrows are raised in surprise. "Fuck, Mouse. That's awesome. Congratulations, buddy."

Mouse nods. "Thank you."

"It's settled then. Tomorrow night. Everybody's going." I stare at Ryker, eyes wide at his declaration. "We'll just move the party from the clubhouse to the bar. It'll be fun." He smirks, walking out of the garage.

Watching him go, I feel anxiety creeping into my mind. A date means she's going to expect romance and shit. I don't know how to be fucking romantic. This is bullshit. If it were anyone else but Ryker, I'd tell them to go fuck themselves, but I owe Ryker my life.

Over a year ago, back when he'd found me in that bar, I was angrier than I am now. My life had been hard and there was no sign of it ever getting any better. When I turned eighteen, I was released from juvie on probation and sent off into the world with no family and no support. I spent the next eight years doing any job I could get my hands on just to keep myself fed. I worked in a grocery store, and a farm, security at a mall, and fought in every underground fight I could get in on. Most of my money came from bouncing, though.

Being a bouncer at a bar when you're not social fucking sucks. Everyone either wants to be your new best friend or wants to fucking fight you. I was tired of that job, tired of living that life – of not belonging anywhere. When Ryker told me about the Kings, it gave me something I hadn't experienced in a long fucking time. *Hope*. Hope for a future. Hope for a family. Hope for finally finding where I was supposed to be.

Now, watching his back as he stalks across the parking lot, I lose that hope. He knows I hate this shit. That motherfucker is selling me out for pussy.

Jase and Mouse laugh again. "Fuck, Tease. It's not the end of the fucking world." Jase wipes the tears that are streaming down his face. "Your girl is fuckin' hot! Show her off!" He makes an attempt to look serious. "It'll be fun! I won't be bringing anyone, but I'll be there."

Mouse cocks his head to the side. "Why won't you bring someone?"

Jase wags his eyebrows. "Keepin' my options open."

Smiling, Mouse shakes his head. "Well, Sarah and I will be there. I've been wanting to introduce her to everyone anyways." Outnumbered and annoyed, I pick up a wrench and start working on putting a new part on the motor. Not knowing when to shut the fuck up, Mouse keeps talking. "I'm glad you worked shit out with Laynie." *Jesus.* The man is asking for a fist in the face. "I think she's good for you."

Standing from my crouch on the floor, I stalk over to Mouse, gathering his t-shirt in my fist as I pull him off his feet. "You gonna put your fuckin' pussy away and come fix this bike or what?"

Eyes wide, he nods.

"Good." I drop him, walking back to the bike, the sound of Jase's laughter rings through the garage. *Bastard.*

Laynie

My pulse is racing as we walk up to the entrance to The Pig's Ear. I've never been to a bar before, but I've been looking forward to tonight all week. Stopping, I ask Travis for the third time, "How do I look?"

He growls and comes to a stop, pulling my body into his. "For the third fuckin' time, you look sexy as hell. Relax."

I smile widely, bouncing on the tips of my toes. "I can't! I'm excited!"

"Fuckin' nut," he mutters as he brushes his lips against mine. He sighs. "Let's do this."

Grinning, I follow Travis, our hands clasped tightly together as we walk into the bar. It's a little nerve-wracking being out in public without Dexter, but I can tell that it means a lot to Travis that I trust him to guide me. Dexter deserves the night off anyway.

The noise of the people and the music hits me as soon as the door opens. The place is packed. Together, we maneuver through the crowd. The combined smells of alcohol and perfume make my nose twitch.

"Laynie! Tease! Over here!" Charlotte. My heart warms, hearing her sound just as excited as I feel.

Travis slows and places my hand on the back of a tall chair, a clear indication for me to sit. I climb up on the stool and smooth down my short skirt just as a pair of arms wrap themselves around me.

"Oh, I'm so glad you made him bring you!" Charlotte squeals in my ear.

I hug her back. "I didn't give him a choice." Pulling back, I wink and grin.

I hear a couple of chuckles from close by and tilt my head slightly. "So, who's here?"

"Right!" Charlotte leans in closer. "Tease is behind you. On your left side is Reaper, then Jase, then Mouse and Sarah, then back around to Ryker and me!"

Waving, I grin. "Hi everyone."

After a round of grunts, heys and hey Barbie's, everyone goes back to their conversations. "What are you drinkin'?" Travis asks from behind me.

I turn in my chair and smile at him. "Wine?"

He scoffs. "Not here you're not. They serve beer and hard shit. Take your pick."

Not happy with that, I stick out my lower lip in a mock pout and turn toward Charlotte. "What are you having, Charlotte?"

"It's Charlie, and I'm drinking rye and ginger. It takes some getting used to, but it's good!"

Turning back to Travis, I nod. "I'll have what she's having."

"Jesus," he mutters as he moves away.

Ignoring him and his party pooper tendencies, I turn to my left anxious to get to know Travis's friends. "Reaper was it?"

"Yeah." His voice is full of grit and gravel. He sounds sexy.

"I'm assuming that's not your real name?"

"You'd be right."

Wow. Obviously, Reaper is not the chatty type.

I turn and face in the direction I think Mouse is. "Hi, Mouse!"

"Hey, Laynie," he answers, voice full of affection. "Meet my girl, Sarah."

I smile. "Hi, Sarah. I hear congratulations are in order."

Her voice is full of excitement when she answers. "Yes. We're getting married and having a baby."

Surprised, I hold out my hand across the table and smile again. "I heard about the baby, but not about the wedding! That's wonderful. May I feel your ring?"

After she places her hand in mine, I run my thumb across the tiny diamond. "He says he'll get me a bigger one when we can afford it." She sounds embarrassed.

"No! Don't do that!" I squeeze her hand. "It's perfect the way it is! It's a symbol of the beginning for you both. Don't change it."

She squeezes back, warmth in her voice. "Thanks."

I pull back and tilt my head again. "Nice to see you again, Jase."

"You too, Barbie."

Travis returns at that moment with my drink. I take a sip, coughing a little at the strong aftertaste, but decide instantly that Charlie's right. It's delicious. As a group, we sit at our table for hours drinking and laughing and carrying on our separate conversations. Every once in a while, women approach our table, trying to engage Reaper or Jase in conversation. Reaper blows them off rudely while Jase seems to revel in it, though, I notice he never leaves with any of them.

The drinks go down easily, and as the men talk, Sarah, Charlie and I form a new friendship. Sarah is shy and sweet, and obviously in love with Mouse. Charlie is kind and fun to hang out with. My belly aches from the laughter we share as the night wears on.

One of the ladies from Charlie's work shows up at our table, there for a night out with her friends. Her name is Ellen, and though she doesn't stick around long, she invites me and the other two ladies out for a night on the town. Excitement overwhelms me. I'm finally making friends, and for the first time in a long time, I feel like I fit in.

As she walks away, Jase leans in between Charlie and me. "No matter how many times I see it, that ass never fails to get me hard."

Ryker growls. "You mind not talkin' to my old lady about your fuckin' dick, asshole?"

Jase laughs. "I can't help it! That bitch is hot."

"Jase," Charlie says. "Not her. She's my friend, and you can't play her like that. She's a good person."

"I ain't fuckin' playin'! That ass drives me wild!"

Charlie laughs. "Well, that may be, but you need to leave that ass alone."

"Whatever," he mutters as walks away, followed by the sounds of our laughter.

"He's such a dog." Charlie laughs. "Good thing I love him." I hear the ice in her glass clinking against the side, and then she slams it down on the table. "All right girl, let's dance!"

Biting the inside of my lip, I freeze. "Um...I think I'll pass."

"What?" she cries. "Why?"

"I don't want to step on anyone."

"Oh, please! You weigh like a hundred pounds. Besides, the place has died down a lot. Hardly anyone is out there now." She tugs on my arm. "Come on! It'll be fun!"

Unable to resist her enthusiasm, I stand on wobbly legs. *Yep. I'm drunk.*

Travis grabs my hand as Charlie grabs my other and starts to pull me toward the dance floor. "You sure?"

I wink at him. "I'll be OK."

Charlie leads me onto the floor where the heat of the lights makes a sweat break out across my brow. Holding onto both of my hands, I feel the sway of her arms and know she's dancing. "Just move, Laynie."

Nodding, I close my eyes and let my body sway to the music. After a minute, I let go of Charlie's hands, raising my arms high in the air as I swirl my hips in slow sensual circles. I love to dance; I've just never done it in front of anyone in a very long time.

With each song, the sweat grows heavier at the nape of my neck as we bounce and sway and gyrate to the music. I feel sexy and invincible on that dance floor. The whole world fades, except for me and the music.

Strong arms wrap around my waist from behind, the smell of leather surrounding me. "Time to go, babe."

I grind my ass back into him as I dance. "I don't want to go yet."

His arms tighten, his fingertips going inside my shirt to stroke the skin on my belly. "Been watching you dance like this for an hour, Laynie. Can't take it anymore." He grinds his hips into mine, letting me feel his hard length against my ass.

My clit pulses as I grin. "Bye, Charlie!"

I hear her giggle as he pulls me out of the bar.

Tease

IT'S LATE THE next night when I get to Laynie's apartment. I've had a shit day and crawling into bed beside her while she sleeps makes all that shit just drift away – well, most of it, anyways. I need to find a way to tell Laynie more about what's going on with the club and explain to her why she's going to have Mouse following her ass around for the next little while. It's not a conversation I look forward to.

Pushing all that shit to the side, I curl into her back and drag her body tightly into mine, spooning her. My cock wakes right up, hardening when he finds himself nestled right into the crack of her perfectly-formed ass. Fuck me. She's fucking naked – always full of surprises. I don't know if I'll ever get enough of them.

Waking slowly, she inhales and snuggles her body back into me and whispers. "Hi."

"Hi."

"I missed you today."

I say nothing as I wrap my arms around her and squeeze her tight, kissing her lightly on the shoulder.

Rolling her hips, she grinds her ass slowly against my cock. "I really missed you."

Need washes over me. Sliding my palm up her belly, I cup her breast, pinching her nipple between my thumb and forefinger. She gasps and groans softly. Reaching behind me to grip my ass, she pulls me into her as she continues to grind against me slowly.

My palm glides down her belly, feeling her silky smooth skin against the rough callouses on my hand. Reaching her center, I slide my finger down and press against the tiny bud of nerves. She whimpers softly, pressing herself into me as tight as she can while her body trembles with excitement. "Please," she whispers.

I slide my finger down farther — collecting her juices – and slide it back up to her clit, circling it slowly. She moans, reaching up and pinching her own nipples tightly. "Please, Travis." Her head tilts back, her teeth clamped down tightly on her bottom lip. I can't take my fucking eyes off her. She looks so fucking sexy like that, riding my hand, touching her own breasts and begging for me.

I work my finger faster, needing to get her there because I need to be inside of her more than I need to breathe. When her finger slides down over my own, I almost lose it. Her other hand comes up and reaches back, sliding up the back of my head, pulling my face down to hers.

Our mouths mash together in a frenzy, tongues tangling together while we writhe on the bed. She continues to rub her clit while I thrust first one, then a second finger deep inside of her. She cries out, teeth clamping onto my lower lip while her orgasm consumes her.

Reaching down, I position my throbbing cock at her entrance and drive up inside of her. She cries out again, her muscles clamping down on my dick with her orgasm. "You fuckin' feel that, Laynie?"

I pound into her, the pleasure taking over my own body. Laynie pants and screams with each of my thrusts, reaching back and digging her fingernails into my ass. "Yes!" she cries.

Knowing this isn't going to last very fucking long if I stay in this position, I pull out and flip her to her belly. Grabbing her hips, I drag her up so her ass is pulled high in the air. Slamming inside, I grit my teeth. "That's me fuckin' owning you. You're mine, Laynie."

"I am," she pants. "I'm yours, baby."

I lose myself to her, the sounds of her cries tattooing themselves on my brain. Lost to the pleasure of being inside Laynie, I'm not thinking when I bring my hand down on her ass with a loud smack.

She freezes beneath me, bringing me out of my fog. "Oh fuck. Lay-nie…fuck! I'm so sorry."

"Do it again," she breathes.

"What?"

"Do it again."

Unsure if she really means it, I raise my hand and bring it down on her smooth skin once more, lightly.

She growls. "I said fucking do it again, Travis!"

Raising my hand once more, I bring it down with a loud smack. Her pussy tightens, and she moans, rocking her hips back into me. Fuck. This woman is fucking incredible.

Grabbing her by the hips, I thrust into her again, grinding my hips into her ass with each thrust. I bring my hand up and slap her ass once more. She growls and thrusts back onto me, nearly knocking me back onto my ass. She's fucking magnificent.

"Mine," I growl as my orgasm tears through me then, my entire body trembling. Slowing my thrusts, I slide my hand up her back to the nape of her neck where I grab her hair and pull her up so her back is pressed against my chest.

Taking her mouth with my own, I kiss her, hoping she can feel what I feel for her in that kiss, because I want her to know but have no idea how to tell her.

Laynie

Travis settles on the bed, and I follow him, nestling into the crook of his arm and resting my head on his chest as we both attempt to catch our breath.

"Wow," I whisper, trying to wrap my head around what had just happened.

He chuckles. "Fuck yeah."

I smile, planting a kiss on his pec. We lie in silence: me stroking the skin of his chest with my thumb, him playing with my hair. can't believe we're finally here, lying like this, together – and happy I know we still have a long way to go, and I still have a lot to learn about Travis, but hearing him declare me as "mine" was it for me. *am* his, and I want to stay that way.

"Laynie?"

His voice pulls me from my thoughts. "Hmmm?"

"We gotta talk."

His gruff voice is filled with apprehension, crashing the wave of contentment I was riding to pieces. "OK."

"Remember I told you the club was dealin' with some shit right now?"

I think back. "Yeah. You said it was done."

His hand goes back to sifting through my hair once more. "Well it's not." He sighs. "Look, it's a long fuckin' story, and I'll tell you... eventually. What you need to know now is, we have another club and a pretty pissed off street gang looking to put an end to the Kings."

I freeze, fear and anger making my blood boil. "Are these the same people who ran us off the road?"

He squeezes me tightly to him. "The very same. It's not safe for us right now, but we're aware, and we're watching. I'm not worried about that." Gripping my chin between his thumb and forefinger, he tips my head back so he can see my face. "But I *am* worried about you."

Fighting back the urge to roll my eyes, I reach forward and aim for his mouth, giving him a brush of my lips. "Don't you worry about me, honey. I can take care of myself."

He squeezes my chin. "Not against two pissed off gangs you can't. These are bad people, Laynie. *Very* bad. They don't want to hurt you. They want to kill you because of me."

Shit. That sounds serious. "Maybe we can go to Daniel?"

"Fuck, no!" he growls.

I prop myself up on my elbow. "Why *not*? I mean, he's a cop right? He can help."

He groans. "Babe, I'm gonna let you in on a little secret. Bikers nd cops don't get along."

"Yeah, but if it's about me he can keep his mouth shut, and he can help take care of the problem."

"We go to the cops, a lot of us will end up in jail. We're not exactly upstanding citizens, Laynie."

"What does that mean?"

"It means we do a lot of shit that's not exactly legal, and the cops would love to get their hands on us."

My eyes narrow. "You know, I think I'm ready to hear at least part of that long story now. I can't wait for *eventually*. What does your club do that the cops could put you in jail for?"

He doesn't answer me. I wait, praying that he will trust me with this – that he trusts me enough to tell me something so big.

He huffs out a big breath. "Well, the Kings used to be into some pretty crazy shit. Gunner and Ryk have worked hard to clean that shit up. Mostly, we grow and distribute weed. We sell medical-grade marijuana and provide it to almost every dealer in this part of the province. We also have a few side businesses. Jase runs the garage, and we have another guy who runs six different dance clubs here in the city. We also own three strip clubs."

"That's it?" My shoulders slump with relief. "I thought you were going to tell me you ran guns or killed people for hire. I can handle weed and strip clubs."

He chuckles softly.

"So what are we going to do?" I ask.

Groaning, he slams his mouth down onto mine, kissing me until my head swims. Pulling back, he whispers. "You don't know how fuckin' happy I am that you're not gonna fight me on this shit."

I crinkle my nose. "Why would I fight you?"

"Because you're a fuckin' smartass. Anyways, Mouse is going to shadow you for a while. Just 'til we know it's safe."

Confused, I tilt my head to the side. "What do you mean by shadow me?"

"He goes everywhere you go when I'm not with you."

Groaning, I nod in defeat. "Fine. But this better not be a long-term thing. I like Mouse, but I don't know if I can handle him being with me all the time. I like my quiet time."

Travis leans in, nuzzling my ear. "I know, babe. It's not forever."

I nod, wondering if being a biker's old lady is always going to be this dangerous. As I snuggle back down into Travis's arms, I realize that even if it is, that's OK by me.

Laynie

AFTER A LONG day of shopping and laughing, my heart is full of love for Charlie. In just the short time I've known her, I finally feel like someone actually likes me and that my blindness doesn't matter to them. My hands are full of shopping bags, my belly hurts from laughing, and my legs need a rest from walking.

"Do you want to stop at the coffee shop for a cup before we go home?" Charlie asks.

Smelling the sweet smell of chocolate and coffee in the air, I smile. "Sounds like a good idea."

Mouse groans behind us. "Fuck me. I thought we were goin' home now."

"Come on, Mouse," I call, walking into the shop behind Charlie. "I'll buy you a hot chocolate for being such a good boy." I wink at him.

"A white hot chocolate?" he asks hopefully.

I laugh. "You got it."

After getting our hot drinks, we go outside to the patio. As we take our seats, Mouse declares, "I'm takin' the dog across the road for a leak."

Charlie and I laugh as he walks away. "Poor Mouse is getting tired of shopping," Charlie says.

I nod. "Yeah, he's been a good sport until now, though."

She laughs again. "Yeah, except when we were in the sex shop. He did not enjoy watching us feel up all the dildos."

We roar with laughter.

"Who stays with you when Ryker's away?" I ask her.

"Another prospect. His name's Bosco." She pauses, and I hear her blowing on her coffee. "He's OK, but like someone else we know, he doesn't have much to say."

"I haven't met him yet."

"To be honest, I kind of miss Tease. He was broody, but we kind of got used to each other, you know?"

I nod.

"How are things with you two anyways?" she asks.

I grin. "Really great, actually. He still doesn't talk much, but he's opening up. He's awesome, actually."

"Good, honey. I'm glad." I can hear the smile in her voice. "He's lucky to have found you."

I shake my head. "No. I'm the lucky one. My life was so boring before I met him, but I didn't even know it. Now I have friends and a hot boyfriend, and a bodyguard named Mouse."

She snorts and laughs. "Right." She's silent a moment. "Mine was far from boring, but it was scary as hell. Most of all, it was just lonely. Then Ryker came along and opened up a whole new world to me."

I smile. "Sounds like one of my books."

She sighs. "It does, doesn't it? It wasn't easy at first, and we almost didn't make it, but now...I never knew life could be so good." She chuckles. "Rival gangs notwithstanding."

I smile wistfully. "I hope Travis and I have that someday."

"You will," she declares. "Your man is hot as hell, and he actually talks to you which is more than he does with most people. He's into you."

I grin wickedly, wagging my eyebrows. "He is hot. Those abs on that man make my mouth run dry."

Charlie giggles. "His eyes are incredible too."

I sigh. "He calls himself a monster."

"A monster!" she exclaims. "Because of that scar on his face?" I nod. "Girl, that scar just makes him hotter. The only thing scary about Tease is his attitude. He works hard to make people afraid of him, but it has nothing to do with his face."

Just then, Mouse comes back with Dexter, flopping down into the seat beside mine. "What are we talkin' about?"

I grin. "How hot Travis is."

He groans. "Gross. Can we just fuckin' go already? Sarah's been blowin' up my fuckin' phone with texts, and I need to see to my woman."

Charlie and I laugh and stand. Grabbing Dexter's harness, I nudge him on the way by. "All right, Mouse. Since you asked so nicely."

"Damn right," he says, clearly proud of himself. Charlie and I laugh, leaving him to walk several feet behind us carrying our shopping bags.

Tease

Using the shiny new key Laynie gave me, I let myself into her apartment. She's not back from her shopping trip with Charlotte yet, so I take off my boots, grab a beer from the fridge, and flop down on the couch to watch some TV. Settling on a show full of bearded men hunting alligators, I look around the room.

My place is a fucking shit pit compared to Laynie's. Her place is decorated, homey, and smells good. Mine has a bed, a chair, and a gun case in the closet. And it smells like fucking feet. We've only been together a few short weeks, but I like seeing my boots beside her pink running shoes and long brown high-heeled boots. I like seeing my black clothes tangled up on the floor with her pink ones, and my toothbrush sharing a holder with hers.

I want this. I want to come home every night to "our" place where it's decorated with pink fucking flowers and smells like apple pie. I want to come home each night and flop down on "our" couch and watch TV with her snuggled on my lap and crawl into bed be side her, making her call out my name at the end of a long day.

The phone rings, the caller ID telling me out loud that it's Laynie's mother calling...again. The woman never stops. Ignoring the phone, I let it ring and turn back to the TV, watching the crazy fuck on the screen roll a gigantic gator into his boat, its tail still thrashing.

Five minutes later, the phone rings again. This time, Laynie's mother leaves a message. Her voice echoes throughout the apart ment.

"Laynie Marie Lawson! I don't know what you're trying to prove, but I'm getting sick of it. I've been trying to call you all day It's important! I don't know if you are trying to punish me, or if that criminal you're dating has stuffed your dead body in a freezer! I'm worried! Call me back as soon as you get this."

Fuck me. I don't know how Laynie's put up with that woman for this long. She's fucking relentless. I assume that I have Laynie's pig brother to thank for her mother hating me already, sight unseen. Shaking my head, I grit my teeth and finish my beer.

Not even ten minutes later, the phone rings again. This time, I haul my ass off the couch and answer it. Bringing it to my ear, I grind out, "Hello?"

Silence. Then I get, "Who is this?"

I roll my eyes. "Travis."

"I need to speak with Laynie."

"She's not here. But I'll tell her you called...again." I grit my teeth, forcing myself to be respectful to her. She is Laynie's mother and I haven't even met her yet. No need to piss her off before that nightmare comes true.

"What do you mean she's not there? If she's not there, why are you?"

I sigh heavily. "Look, Laynie's out shopping with a friend. She'll be home soon, and I will let her know you called."

"Laynie doesn't go shopping. She can't *see*. And she doesn't *have* any friends. She has *me*, and her father, and her brother."

Gripping the phone tightly in my hand, I keep my voice as ever as I can. "And she has *me*, and a whole new group of friends who do things like take her shopping and help her out when she fucking needs it." I blow out a frustrated breath. "Look, lady, no disrespect, but you need to cut the fuckin' cord." Her shocked gasp doesn't faze me a bit. "Laynie's a grown ass woman. She can *more* than take care of herself. Now if you don't mind, I've got some gators to watch."

I hang up, just as she starts to speak. Tossing the phone down onto the table, I turn to go back to the couch when I see Laynie standing in the doorway, arms full of shopping bags, and Mouse standing behind her smirking.

"Was that my mom?" she asks.

"Yeah." I watch her closely, unsure of how she's going to react to me telling off her mother.

Her wonky grin appears on her face, nearly knocking me on my ass. Tossing her bags off to the side, she turns and takes the bags from Mouse. "Beat it, Mouse." His face is full of shock just as she shuts the door in his face.

I stare at her eyebrows raised as she walks toward me. When she starts to walk too far to the left, I call out, "I'm over here, babe."

She smirks and corrects her course. When she gets close enough, I reach out, grabbing onto her hand to pull her into me. Pressing her hand into my chest, she smiles brightly up toward my face. "That was fucking hot."

"Hotter than me bein' a biker like some lame asshole in your books?"

She shakes her head. "Nope. But close."

My laugh is cut off when she grabs my face, yanking it down and crushing her lips to mine, her tongue forcing its way into my mouth. Her kiss is rough and hungry, and every ounce of blood in my body rushes straight to my dick. Her tits rub against my chest, and I need to see them. Not caring about the shirt she's wearing, I yank it open, tearing buttons fling across the room. I pull back and watch as her chest heaves with excitement.

Yanking the cups of her bra down, her tits are presented to me like a fucking feast ready to be devoured. I growl, dipping my head to catch one of her nipples between my lips, tugging gently. She groans and spears her fingers into my hair.

"Travis," she pants. I flick my tongue across her nipple and rub her clit roughly through her jeans. "Travis, stop." I fumble with the button on her jeans. "Travis." She shoves my hands away. "Stop!"

Confused, I jerk back and stare at her.

She reaches toward me, sliding her fingers across my hips until she finds my belt buckle. "It's my turn," she whispers.

Heart hammering, my eyes widen as she drops to her knees in front of me. Reaching forward, she slowly pulls down the zipper o my jeans and pulls them down over my hips, leaving them to wrap around my ankles. My hard cock bounces in front of her, ready to play whatever game she has in mind.

I watch as her pink tongue creeps out, sliding across her plump lips, moistening them and making them shine. Her palms glide up my legs until she reaches the part of me that is aching with need. Hesitantly, she wraps her hand around the base of my cock, making my eyes roll back in my head.

Looking down on her, I bite the inside of my lip, willing myself not to cum in her hand. She's on her knees, tits still out, propped up with her bra, her blond hair falling all around her shoulders as she softly slides her hand up my shaft.

My breath catches in my throat. When she leans forward, her tongue slides out, and she flattens it, dragging it slowly up the underside of my cock before she pulls away. *Fuck.* I grip her hair with my fingers, pulling her back in. Using her hand, she guides me back to her mouth, wrapping her lips around the tip and sucking hard swirling it quickly with her tongue.

My knees nearly buckle. Taking me deeper, she licks and sucks my dick until the pleasure starts to feel almost like pain. I stare down at her, watching her take my cock. When she slides me inside her mouth as far as she can go and moans, I can't take it anymore.

"Babe. You gotta stop."

Using her hand to stroke me as she bobs her head up and down sucking my dick like a fucking lollipop, she ignores me.

"Babe," I rasp.

She pulls away. "Cum, honey."

My orgasm rocks me back on my heels as I cum into her mouth. We moan together, me trembling, and her sucking and swallowing down every last drop from my dick. When I sigh, exhausted and spent, she pulls away and licks her lips before turning her face to mine and smiling her wonky smile. "Now it's your turn."

Chuckling, I lift her off the floor and carry her off to the bedroom.

Tease

JASE STANDS FROM where he was crouched down beside my bike, wiping his hands on a rag. "There ya go, fuckface. Good as new."

I smirk, thankful that I don't have to drive the club's van anymore. "Thanks, man."

Jase jerks and makes a face, clutching his chest with one hand. "Jesus Christ, man. A smirk? What has that bitch done to you?"

Rolling my eyes, I walk around the bike, checking out his handiwork. "Fuck off and move. Takin' her for a tour, make sure you fuckin' fixed her for sure."

"Oh, she's fixed. Enjoy, brother." I put my helmet on my head and am fastening the strap when he speaks again. "You hear about the picnic next weekend?"

I pause. *Picnic? We're in the middle of a goddamned war with the Devils, and he's talking about a picnic?* "No."

"Gunner just told me this mornin'. Apparently since it's starting to get colder, his old lady thought it would be a good time to enjoy the last of summer and relax for a day by the lake." He shrugs. "We haven't heard shit from the Devils, and the Crips don't even have us on their radar. They seem to think the Bloods shot up their men."

I shake my head. "I don't like it. Too easy."

Jase folds his arms across his chest and purses his lips. "Yeah. I guess. I don't know, though. A day to unwind, drink beer, and talk my way into a threesome sounds fuckin' perfect right about now."

I turn the key, starting up my bike and the motor roars throughout the garage. "Maybe, but I'll be on alert. I don't think the Devils are done with us. Not after we killed those fuckers." I swing my leg over the seat and sit down. "Just don't think it's a good idea."

Jase shrugs as I pull out of the garage and onto the street. The bike sounds fuckin' sexy as hell. I can't wait to get her out on the highway where I can put her through the actual test, and see if this bitch can fly as fast as she used to.

Driving through the city, I let my mind wander back to this morning and the conversation I'd had with Laynie. It had been more of an argument in the end, but once again, I think I owe my girl an apology.

We'd been lying in bed, half-asleep, her hand wandering along my abs. "Travis?" she'd asked.

"Hmm?"

"Have you ever seen your mom since you ran away all those years ago?"

My heart clenched. "Just once. After the police found me livin' on the street, she came to the police station. She didn't even look at me. I heard her tell them that I was a delinquent and that she didn't fuckin' want me ruinin' her life anymore. She walked outta there without lookin' back. I haven't seen her since."

"Are you angry with her?" she asked softly.

I scowled and shook my head. "Nope. I just hate the bitch."

"That's sad. Hatred is a poison, Travis."

I sat up, reaching for my jeans. "Don't fuckin' tell me that I need to forgive that bitch, Laynie. She can rot in fuckin' hell for all I care."

She climbed off the bed behind me, stumbling over my motorcycle boot when she took a step. I caught her arm just in time. "That's not what I'm saying." She shook her head and sat back down on the bed. "I'm saying that maybe you're still angry with her, and that causes that hatred. You still care. Maybe, if you can let that anger go, you can finally heal."

I finished buckling up my jeans and jabbed a finger at her. "Don't you even fuckin' bother talkin' your fuckin' therapy shit to me. I've healed just fuckin' fine. This is who I am and I'm not changin'. Not for you. Not for *anyone*."

Yanking my t-shirt over my head, I grabbed my keys and stormed out of the room. Just as I slammed my way out of her apartment, I heard her voice from the bedroom calling out to me. "I don't want you to change, Travis. I want you to be finally be happy."

I'd ignored her, and I'd left. Now, looking back, I should have fucking talked to her. I should have shut my mouth and actually listened to her. I don't give a shit about my mother, but maybe letting go of that hatred would silence the screams I hear in my head sometimes. I *am* angry. Look at how I treated Laynie. She doesn't deserve that shit.

I'm an asshole.

Turning my bike onto the highway, I open her up, and am thrilled to see that Jase has not only fixed my bike, but he's improved it. I fly down the road, passing cars and watching the world float by, and try to come up with a way to apologize to my girl, who I've hurt yet again.

Laynie

Mouse leads me into the clubhouse bar and helps me get settled onto a high barstool and hands me a beer.

"Thanks, Mouse."

"You're welcome. I hate to leave you here, but Sarah has a doctor's appointment, and I can't miss it. Jase said Tease is just out for a rip on his new and improved bike but should be back any time."

I smile and wave him away. "Don't worry about it! Go! See to your girl and your baby." Planting a quick kiss on my cheek, Mouse runs out the door.

I sit back and sip on my beer, listening to the sounds in the room to determine if anyone's nearby. The place is silent. My mind begins to wander, and I think back to the argument I had with Travis this morning.

I'm not angry with him for walking out like he did — I should never have pushed him. From experience, I know that he will deal with those issues when he's ready. I'm not sorry for bringing it up, though. He needed the push to start thinking about his mother. There's no way that bitch doesn't play a part in the man he's become. I don't want him to change – in fact, I like him broody. It's hot as hell. I just don't want him to feel the torture of the mind that goes into hating someone like that. I meant it when I said it's a poison.

"For fuck's sake. Are they just gonna start movin' all their bitches in here now?" Lost in thought, I'd missed her approach, but her bitchy words yank me back into the present.

"Excuse me? Do I know you?"

"Fuck no! Thank God." I hear her step in front of where I sit. "You're Tease's new bitch?"

Who the fuck is this girl? "I'm his girlfriend, yes. Who the fuck are you?"

She laughs. "Lucy. I'm sure you've heard of me. I'm a favorite around here."

I frown and change position, ready to jump up and kick some ass if the need arises. "Oh, right. Lucy. You're the whore."

I hear her heels on the tile floor as she comes at me, but Dexter's growl stops her short. Jumping up, I stand in front of her, fists clenched. I've never been in a fight before, but after hearing Charlie's stories about this girl, I look forward to kicking her skanky ass.

"Fuck you!" she shrieks. "Fuckin' blind bitch, comin' in here and takin' yet another one of my fuckin' men."

I laugh. "You're fuckin' crazy, you know that?" I put my hands on my hips and lean forward. "And there's no way in hell that my man put his dick anywhere near any of *your* rotten holes. I can fuckin' smell the fish from here." I curl my nose in disgust.

I feel her hand in my hair before Dex even gets a chance to warn me. Yanking on my ponytail, she drags my head back. It hurts like a son-of-a-bitch, and I don't get to find out what planned to do next because my punch to her face makes her wail like a baby and release me.

"You fuckin' bitch! You broke my nose," she wails.

I aim my glare in her direction, hoping I look tough, and she can't see the agony I'm in at the moment. Dexter continues to bark so I have to yell to be heard. "Get the fuck out of here before I let my dog at you, you filthy bitch."

I hear her shoes as she runs from the room sobbing. As her foot steps fade, I hear a slow clap coming from the other side of the room. Turning my head in that direction, I tighten my grasp on Dex's harness. "Who's there?"

Heavy footsteps approach me. "Relax. It's just me. Reaper. And might I say, that was fuckin' incredible."

I feel the flush race across my cheeks, knowing that he watched that. "Sorry if she's your...whore, or whatever."

He laughs, and I hear him rifling with something behind the bar "That bitch ain't my anything."

"Did you catch the whole show?"

"Nope. I came when I heard the dog barkin'." He grabs my hand shoving a bag of ice into it. "That'll help with the swelling."

I laugh and gingerly place the ice across my aching knuckles "Thanks. That fucking hurt."

He chuckles and comes around to my side of the bar. "Was about to intervene when she grabbed your hair, but that punch you gave her made me stop and let you deal with her yourself. It was a lesson she needed to learn."

I bite my lip and nod. "So I hear. Charlie told me all about her."

He chuckles again. "I'm sure she did. Charlie should have caved her face in months ago. You should give her lessons."

I laugh. "I'll think about it."

"Gotta admit, I was surprised your dog let her get that far."

I reach down and pat Dex on the head. "He's a lover, not a fighter. He's trained to warn me, and if I give the command, then he'll attack."

"Mind if I pet him?"

I motion to Dex. "Be my guest." I hear the tags on Dex's chain jingle as Reaper rubs him down.

"I used to have a dog."

I cock my head to the side. "Used to?"

More jingling. "Yeah. In Afghanistan. Fuckin' thing came up to me one day while I was out on patrol with my troop. Wouldn't fuckin' leave." He pauses. "He was so fuckin' skinny. I knew he was starvin'. Started givin' him half of my meals, and he became my new patrol buddy. I named him Monty."

I hear the creak from his leather cut as he sits back, followed by the sounds of him swallowing and setting down a bottle of, what I can only assume, is beer. "That stupid dog became my new best friend. Saved my fuckin' life more times than I can count. I couldn't bring him onto base, but he was always at the gate waitin' for me when we left. He'd wag his fuckin' tail so hard I thought his ass was gonna come right off."

He chuckles, lost in the memory. "Then one day, we went out on a mission. We were walkin' through the desert, comin' close to one of the towns we needed to check on, and just as I went to take a step, Monty freaked the fuck out, ran right at me, knockin' me right to my back. I was pissed. I got up to give the little fucker shit when he took a stumbled back right where I'd been about to step, and he was gone. Just...gone."

Horrified, I swallow, running my fingers through Dexter's fur. "What happened to him?" I whisper, afraid I already know the answer.

"Improvised explosive device." He takes another long swig of his beer, slamming the bottle back down on the counter. "Fucker blew up."

I clap my hands over my mouth. "No!"

Before he can respond, more footsteps come into the room. "What the fuck, Reaper? What are you doin' to my girl?"

"Fuck you, Tease. We were just talkin'," he growls.

"Then why does she look like she's about to fuckin' cry?"

I stand quickly, throwing my hands up in the air. "It's fine,

Travis. We were just talking and he told me a sad story. That's all."

Travis says nothing, and I hear Reaper's chair scrape across the floor as he stands. "See ya later, Laynie. Take care of that dog."

I smile. "Will do. And Reaper?"

He pauses as he exits the room, but says nothing.

"Thank you for sharing that story with me."

He grunts and walks out.

"What the fuck was that all about," Travis asks.

I smile up at him, molding my body to his. "Just a story about a dog he once had. It had a sad ending." I bury my face in his neck. "Are you still mad at me?"

He shakes his head and squeezes me tight. "Fuck no. You mad at me?"

I kiss his neck, and whisper, "No."

"Why is there ice on your hand?"

"I punched Lucy in the face. Think I broke her nose too."

He grabs my hand to inspect it for himself. "That bitch was botherin' you?" he growls.

"Not anymore," I say with a wink.

Bringing my hand to his lips, he kisses it softly and chuckles. "That's my girl."

Eighteen

Laynie

IT'S THE DAY of the picnic, and I can't wait to get back on that motorcycle. It's about a two-hour drive to the lake and Mouse has already left in the van with Dexter and my huge bowl of potato salad. After grabbing my bikini and a towel, I'm ready to go.

"Would you stop fuckin' bouncin'?" Travis growls, trying to do up my helmet.

"I can't help it! I'm excited!" Forcing myself to stand still, he finally gets the strap done up. "I've been looking forward to this all week."

"It's a fuckin' picnic, Laynie. Not a damned circus."

"Oh, don't be such a grouch. Besides, it's not the picnic I'm excited about. It's the ride there." I lean forward and press my lips against his. "I can't wait to get my man between my legs again."

He growls and cups my ass, pulling me into him. "Keep talkin' like that and we won't be goin' anywhere but the fuckin' bedroom."

Giggling softly, I shove his shoulder lightly. "Behave. I need a tan and a swim and a fully-loaded hamburger, stat."

"I'll give you a—"

"Stop!" I cry, throwing my hand up in the air. "Let's just go."

Chuckling, Travis helps me onto the bike before swinging onto it himself. As we pull out onto the street, I revel in the feel of the late summer sunshine beating down on my face. I know we've hit the city limits and the open road when Travis picks up speed, causing my heart to soar with joy. I'll never get enough of riding this bike with him. I'll never get enough of *him*.

Since meeting Travis a couple of months ago, my life has changed so much. I have friends and laughter, and best of all, sex. Lots and lots of incredible, toe-curling sex. My brother and I have grown farther apart, but I have faith that our relationship can be fixed. My mother has backed off a lot since Travis had words with her. I want her to meet him – to see that I'm OK. I never want to hurt my mom, but Travis was right when he told her to cut the cord.

The best change has been Travis himself. He's gruff, and sometimes he can be a total asshole, but he's also protective, and sweet and I know that my blindness doesn't bother him in the least. I've noticed a change in him. He's almost happy sometimes, and I like to think I have at least something to do with that. I've come so close to telling him I love him so many times, but I've stopped myself. I'm afraid that he'll feel trapped and that he's not ready for that yet, so I keep it inside. But I do – I love him. I love him so much my heart aches in the best possible way.

Travis slows, pulling to a stop and cutting the motor. Climbing off the bike, he takes my hand in his and helps me to stand beside it. "How was that?"

I beam. "Amazing. I could ride all day if I was with you."

Wrapping his arms around my waist, he pulls me tightly to him and claims my mouth with his own. The sounds of the others laughing and talking in the background fade as I drape my arms around his neck and pour all of my love for him into that kiss. Our tongues slide against one another and my heart stutters in my chest when he pulls away and grabs my face in both of his huge hands.

"I fuckin' love you, Laynie Lawson."

My belly dips and my breath catches before it even leaves my chest. "You do?"

He leans in and kisses me again, nipping at my lower lip. "Fuck yeah."

Joy washes over me as I revel in the feeling of his words warming me from the inside out. "I love you too, Travis. So much. I wanted to tell you before, but I was afraid I'd scare you away."

Positioning his lips above mine, he whispers, "Not gonna happen."

Hearing a familiar bark, I turn just in time to pet Dexter as he reaches me. Travis takes me by the hand, leading me to the group of carefree bikers and their families, introducing me to those I haven't met yet.

The afternoon is filled with laughter and beer and making new friends. I also get the not-so-great pleasure of meeting Tiny. The guy is a complete dick, and I instantly dislike him. I can tell from the way Travis stands in front of me that he can't stand him either. When Gunner calls Travis away, he leaves me sitting in the shade with Dexter and Tiny not so far away.

"Nice dog you got there, Leanne."

I smirk. "It's Laynie. And thank you."

I hear the crunch of grass beneath his feet as he takes a step closer. "Mind if I pet him?"

Before I get a chance to answer, Dexter presses close to my leg, and his growl rumbles through his whole body. Shocked, I place my hand on his head. "That might not be a good idea."

"Ah, it'll be fine. Come here, mutt. I won't hurt ya."

Dexter's growl gets louder and his body trembles against my leg. Suddenly, he lets out a vicious bark followed by Tiny's loud yelp of surprise. "Stupid fuckin' dog. I'll kick you right in the fuckin' head!"

He comes closer again. Squaring my shoulders, I open my mouth to tell him just where he can go fuck himself, when Reaper brushes past me. "You fuckin' come anywhere near this dog, or Laynie, again I'll rip your tiny fuckin' dick off and feed it to Dexter here as a fuckin' snack."

Smirking, I wait for him to argue and am surprised when he just tosses out a hate-filled, "Fuck you," before walking away.

The rest of the afternoon, I swim with Charlie and lounge on the sand where we laugh hysterically as I describe my encounter with Lucy the other day. "Man, I wish I could have been there to see the look on her face!" she squeals between bouts of laughter.

"She said I broke her nose," I giggle. "My hand hurt like a son-of-a-bitch afterward, though.

She laughs. "I bet. I could never hit someone."

I point at her, growing serious. "That's why she got to you last time. You need to set that bitch straight. From what you told me, you did absolutely nothing, and that's not OK. Us ladies, we need to stick together, not make things more difficult."

She sighs. "I know. I just hate confrontation. Besides, you haven't seen her – Lucy's tough. She'd kick my ass."

"You're right. I can't see her." I smirk. "And I still kicked her ass."

Giggling like a pair of old friends, we lie in the sun and enjoy what's left of the afternoon. After a while, I realize that I haven't seen my dog or Travis in a long time. Sitting up, I listen closely for the sounds of Dexter's tags. "Do you see Dex?"

I hear her move beside me. "Yeah. He's over there, sitting in the shade with Reaper, of all people."

I lie back and smile. "Yeah. Turns out Reaper's a bit of a dog-lover."

"Really?" Her voice is laced with disbelief.

I nod, not willing to say anymore and tell a story that isn't mine to tell.

"Huh," she says. "Who knew?"

As afternoon meets evening and our skin starts to cool, we rush off to the trees and scramble back into our clothes. Stepping out from our makeshift changing room, Charlie leads me back to the group. "Hey, Mouse. Jase. Have you guys seen Ryker?"

"Or Travis?" I add.

"Yeah. They're over by the bikes talkin' to Gunner," Jase replies.

"Great. Thanks. I'll go grab them. You coming, Laynie?"

I shake my head. "Nah. I'll stay here and wait. Travis'll be along soon."

"All right. Suit yourself."

I hear her footsteps as she crunches across the ground and turn to Mouse and Jase. "So, what are we talking about?"

"Tits," Jase answers.

"Jase was talkin' about tits. I was listenin'," Mouse hurries to explain.

"OK," I laugh. "What about tits?"

"Not just *any* tits," Jase replies. "There's a bitch over there, has the biggest fuckin' tits I've ever seen in real life."

I raise my eyebrows. "Exciting."

Jase laughs. "So exciting, I think I may just go over there and introduce myself." I feel the breeze of him walking past me. "If you ladies will excuse me."

"Yeah. Fuck you too, Jase," Mouse calls after him.

Laughing, I turn back to him. "So how did Sarah's appointment go?"

"It was fuckin' amazing." The excitement in his voice warms my heart. "It was her twenty-week ultrasound. Seeing my baby up on that screen was the most beautiful moment of my life."

I smile. "So far."

He chuckles. "Until she gets here, anyways."

"She?"

"Yep. We found out we're having a baby girl!"

I reach for him, clasping his hand in mine. "Oh, Mouse. That's incredible news! I'm so happy for you both."

"Thank you, Laynie." He squeezes my hand. "Sarah had to work today so she couldn't come, but I'll tell her you said that."

I smile brightly up at him. "So, have you guys thought of any names? I hear Laynie is a beautiful name."

He laughs deep in his throat and releases my hand. "Actually, we haven't agreed on one yet. She likes Vivian, and I like Amelia."

I wrinkle my nose. "I'm not a big fan of Vivian, but I love the name Amelia. You could call her Millie!"

"I like tha–"

Suddenly the air fills with the sounds of racing motorcycles and loud pops. "Shit! Laynie, get dow–" Mouse's words are cut off by the sound of a thump as he plows into my front, knocking me to the ground and landing on top of me, causing the wind to rush out of my lungs. Terrified, I lie still, trying to figure out what the hell is going on. The pops continue, coming from two different directions.

"What's going on?" I cry out, but Mouse doesn't answer.

Realizing that the pops are gunshots, I panic. My muscles strain as I push at Mouse, screaming for him to get off me. "Mouse! Move Dexter!"

Unable to breathe, I burst into tears. "Mouse! Move!" I place my hands under him and push on his shoulders. When that fails, I pull my hands away and feel the wetness on them. Lifting it to my nose, my heart constricts when I smell the metallic scent of blood.

"Mouse?" I whisper, my voice trembling as my body begins to shake uncontrollably. "Mouse!" I shake him, hoping to get a reaction.

Lifting my hand, I run it along his back, feeling for the source of the wetness. When I get to his head, the blood is thicker. My lungs wheeze and tears are pouring from my eyes. When my hand touches the higher part of his head and feel nothing but gore where his crown should be, my heart shatters into a million tiny little pieces.

"Nooo!" I shriek. "Help us! Somebody help us! Please!"

The pops continue and I feel the moisture of his blood leaking into my own hair where it spreads on the ground beneath us. Wrapping my arms around him, I cry helplessly, my breaths shallow and fast. I cry for the man I've come to love like a little brother. I cry for the woman whose heart is going to be broken by the loss of this sweet man. And most of all, I cry for the poor unborn baby girl who is going to grow up without her daddy there to rock her to sleep and kiss her goodnight.

Tease

Charlotte had just gotten to us when the shit hit the fan. Every single member of the Devil's Rejects descends on us before we even have a chance to fucking react. There have to be at least thirty of the fuck-

124

rs. They unleash a hail of gunfire on us as we scramble to take cover. Gunner, Ryker, Charlotte, and I duck behind the only cover available – our motorcycles. Pulling out my gun, I return fire. I hear shots coming from Ryker and Gunner and pray that the rest of our brothers have brought their guns as well.

Peering over the top of my ride, I scan the picnic area for Laynie. My heart races to the point of exploding when I don't see her. People are scattered throughout the grounds, hiding behind trees and overturned picnic tables, but I don't see Laynie.

That's when I see Dexter. He's crawling along the ground on his belly. I follow the course he's heading down with my eyes and my gut drops right out from under me. Seeing the prone form of Mouse lying on top of Laynie takes my breath away. *Are they OK?*

"Nooo! Somebody help us! Please!"

Hearing her panicked pleas for help, I jump up from my crouch and start to move in her direction. As I pass Ryker, he grabs my hand and yanks me down beside him and Charlotte. "You fuckin' crazy?"

"Laynie's out there!" I growl and move to stand.

"A lot of people are out there, man! Don't be a fuckin' idiot! Stay put. Mouse has her."

I know he's right, but I don't fucking like it. I reload my gun and fire off more shots, hitting a couple of the Devils and knocking them back. I watch as Dexter makes it to Laynie and stretches out beside her. I see her arm shoot out, wrapping around him and holding him tight to her body. Thankful that he made it to her, and can at least comfort her when I can't, I fire off more shots.

I'm down to my last bullet when the Rejects start jumping on their bikes, and in a deafening roar, make their getaway. Even through all of the shots fired, there are only two of them left on the ground.

Focusing my attention back on Laynie, I run to where she still lies on the ground under Mouse. My heart rattles in my chest as I get closer and see the blood pooled on the ground all around them. Neither of them are moving. The sight of that black pool of blood causes despair to crush the breath from my lungs. I can't breathe.

"Laynie!" I gasp.

Her broken sobs break through my panic. "Travis? Oh God. Help him!"

Kneeling beside them, I freeze when I see Mouse, and it feel like the whole world stops fucking spinning. His skin is grey and there is nothing but gore and blood where the top of his head should be. His eyes are open, but empty of the usual glint he always seem to have. He's gone.

Reaper appears at my side. "Fuck!" he roars.

Laynie's already tear-streaked face crumples, and she starts sobbing uncontrollably. "Help me! Get him off me. Please! I need to get him off me!"

Shaking off the wave of sadness and shock, I grab onto his shoulder, and with Reaper's help, we gently roll him off of Laynie and settle him on the ground beside her. Laynie's shaky hands come up and cover her blood-spattered face as an ear-piercing wail of despair rips from her throat.

Reaching forward, I gather her into my arms, rocking her gently and stroking her hair. Her sobs rack her whole body, ripping my heart to shreds. Sitting on the ground we sway gently while the rest of the group gathers around Mouse. Dex comes over and lies beside us, laying his head on my lap where Laynie is able to pet him while she cries.

I don't know what to do, or what to say. Mouse was a pain in my ass, but fuck me, he was one of the most genuine people I know. He was like a little brother to me, but I never fucking told him that, and that makes me so angry at myself. I was such a dick to him – all the fucking time — but he was always so fucking loyal. *Fuck!*

Just then, Charlotte approaches and kneels beside us, placing a hand on Laynie's shoulder. She flinches and presses herself closer to me. "Laynie?" Her voice shakes, and her chin trembles slightly, but she holds it together. "Honey, it's me, Charlie. Let's go down to the lake and get you cleaned up, sweetheart." She tugs gently on Laynie indicating that she wants her to come with her.

"Nooo," she wails, wrapping herself even tighter around me and hanging on for dear life.

I look at Charlotte and shake my head. She nods, her face filled with sadness, then stands and walks into Ryker's waiting arms, where she too bursts into tears.

Looking around at the silent group of people that I consider family, I rock Laynie from side to side and watch as they all stand in shock and silence. The tightness in my chest is almost unbearable. Jase comes forward and lays a red and white checkered picnic blanket over Mouse's face and then turns, storming away off to his bike.

"Jase!" Ryker calls. "Where are you goin'?"

"I'm goin' to find those sons-of-bitches, and I'm goin' to kill every last fuckin' one of 'em." I've never heard Jase sound so angry, but I agree with him. They are going to pay for this – with their lives. But not yet. First we have to tell Sarah.

Laynie

I DON'T REMEMBER leaving the lake, or the ride home. I don' remember anything but the weight of Mouse's body as his lif poured out of him. My thoughts are clouded, and my stomach i heavy with dread. I can't stop thinking about that thump I'd heard a Mouse was warning me. He'd taken that bullet trying to save my life. I keep thinking about Mouse, and how excited he was to tell me he was having a baby girl. I think about the sincere way he was with everyone, willing to give you the shirt of his back. Mouse was a rare kind of human being, and the loss of him has knocked the wind right out me.

"Come on, babe. Lift your arms." Slowly coming back to the present, I hear the running water of the shower and feel hands at my waist, pulling my blood-soaked t-shirt up and over my head. I raise my arms and fight back the tears as Travis helps me take off the rest of my clothes.

I hear the whisper of fabric as he takes off his own, and then he lifts me into his strong arms, carrying me into the shower and sets me down under the spray of hot water. Blinking, I raise a fist to my chest and press it deep, trying to ease the intense ache I feel.

"Tip your head back, Laynie." Moving on auto-pilot, I do as I'm old and tip my head back under the rushing water. Travis's fingers are gentle but firm as he shampoos my hair, massaging my scalp with strong fingers, washing away the blood and dirt that had caked into it while I was lying on the ground with Mouse.

Wordlessly, he soaps up a loofah and runs it over my body, scrubbing the blood of the sweetest man I know from my skin. My throat stings as a deep, anguished sob bursts from deep inside me, my shoulders shaking with my sorrow.

Travis grabs my shoulders and pulls me close to his body, wrapping me up in his arms. "Fuck, Laynie. I don't even know what the fuck to say to you right now."

I continue to cry, tears coursing down my cheeks, mixing with the stream from the shower. I clutch his shoulders and just let it all out – I need to. I have to get this pain out before it eats me alive. Travis says no more, just holds me tighter, pressing his lips to the top of my head.

Gradually, my tears slow and my breathing evens out. My broken heart remains shattered, but my body is exhausted. Pushing my face against his chest, I press a kiss to his pec. "I'm OK now."

Travis places his hands on each side of my face, lifting it to his and presses his own lips to mine. "You're not, but you're better. Let's get you into bed."

He leans forward to turn off the water and helps me from the shower. I stand still, arms hanging at my side, my body drained of all energy while he carefully dries me off, and after wrapping a large towel around me, he leads me to the bedroom. I stand in the center of the room and wait as I hear him searching for something.

"Here. Put this on."

Raising my arms, I push them through the shirt he's placed over my head. I don't recognize it as one of my own. "What is this?"

"My tee," he answers, pulling me toward the bed. "Love your silky pajamas, babe, but tonight, I need you to wear something of mine."

My chin trembles as I give him a quivery smile. "I love you."

He settles on the bed, pulling me close and hugs me to him tightly. Taking a deep breath through his nose, he breathes out, "Fuck, babe. I love you too."

Wrapping my arm around his waist, I press myself to him as tight as I can get. If I could crawl up inside him, I think I would. Somewhere along the way, Travis has become my safe place, and being wrapped up in a t-shirt that smells like him may just keep the nightmares at bay.

We lie in silence, my chest aching with sadness as I trail my fingertips up and down his arm. "Travis?"

"Yeah." His voice his hoarse.

"Are you OK?"

"Fuck no." His answer surprises me. Not because he feels it, but because he admits to it. "Do you have any idea how fucking terrified I was when I got close to you and saw all that fucking blood?" He lets out a shaky breath. "I thought it was you."

I give him a squeeze but stay silent, waiting for him to continue.

"I think the worst part is, I'm a fucking dick for feeling relief when I found out it wasn't. I was so fucking scared I'd lost you that I felt relief that it was my fucking friend. My *best* fucking friend." His voice rises as he talks, filling with anger. "His fucking head gets blown off saving my woman, and I feel relief? What kind of sick fuck am I?"

I prop myself up on my elbow. "Hey. Don't talk about the man I love that way. What you felt was normal, Travis. Completely normal. You felt relief that it wasn't me, not that he died." Reaching out, I search for his face and press my hand against his scarred cheek. "That doesn't mean you grieve him any less."

He takes a deep breath. "I'm pissed. I'm pissed that those crazy fucks ambushed us and nearly killed us all. I'm pissed that I only got to kill a couple of them. I'm pissed that you had to go through that shit this afternoon. But most of all, I'm pissed at myself. I'm pissed that I never fuckin' told that needy son-of-a-bitch that he was the best fuckin' friend I ever had."

Tears fill my already puffy eyes as I lean forward, pressing my forehead to his. "He knew, honey. He told me once that you were his buddy, even if you hated to admit it." I chuckle softly. "He loved you too, ya know."

Groaning, he pulls me closer and squeezes me tight, whispering, "Yeah. I know."

Tease

t's hard to breathe as I drive in the line-up of motorcycles following he hearse to the cemetery. My throat burns and my heart feels like it weighs a hundred fucking pounds after watching Gunner place Mouse's fully-patched cut into his casket before they closed it, sealing him inside forever. After all his loyalty and hard work, Mouse is finally a patched member of the Kings of Korruption, and he's not even alive to enjoy it.

Laynie and Charlotte are riding with Bosco in the club van, making up the back of the line. I just want to get there and get my girl. Being separated from her, even if it is just riding in separate vehicles, has me fighting to stay calm. Until those fuckers are dead, I don't want to be apart from her.

As we pull up the cemetery road, our motorcycles drowning the silence, I notice a lone unmarked police car parked off to the side of the road. Laynie's brother Daniel stands, in uniform, against the side of the car, eyes pinned on me. *Fuck.*

After the shooting at the lake, the cops had been quick to swoop in. Someone had called them, though we had yet to figure out who that someone was. They'd detained a few of us, including Laynie, and questioned us all. We told them the bare minimum – unknown people had swooped in, shot at us all and then drove away. The cops had found bullet casings that Bosco had missed during his clean up sweep but have yet to connect us to any shooting. We all told them that we didn't know who had shot the two dead Devils that were lying up by the road. They don't believe us, but for the moment, their hands are tied.

Glaring at Daniel as I pass, I walk to the van and reach in to grab Laynie's hand. I help her down and hand Dexter's harness to her, then lead her down to the cemetery plot where Mouse is about to be laid to rest. I don't bother telling her that he's there. She's been a wreck since Mouse died, barely getting any sleep and crying often throughout the day. If she knew that her brother had it out for me, i would break her already fragile heart.

We had decided to have a more casual burial for Mouse, with Gunner officiating. Mouse wasn't religious and aside from Sarah, we were the only family he had. He would have liked this. Sarah sits be side Tess, Gunner's old lady, eyes covered in dark sun glasses, dab bing a tissue underneath them to wipe away the tears from her eyes She clings to Tess's hand like a lifeline.

Gunner stands in front of the casket waiting for us all to get set tled. I look around. The whole club is here, along with old ladies whores, and friends of the club. Mouse would be proud to know tha this many people cared about him. I just wish he'd known that be fore he died.

"Mouse came to me over a year ago wanting a chance to join the Kings. The first time he came, I'd laughed in his face. You could see the kid had a heart the size of Canada beating in his chest, and he wore that heart on his sleeve. These aren't good traits for a King."

He shakes his head, a small smile forming on his face. "We ge kids like Mouse coming into the clubhouse all the time, wanting to be one of us. Wanting to be a tough guy. But they can't hack it Mouse didn't look like he could hack it, either. Kid had a goofy fuckin' grin on his face every time I laid eyes on him. But he proved me wrong."

Looking around at the rest of us, Gunner clears his throat. "Every night he showed up at the clubhouse, and every time he had a new reason of why he would make a good biker. That fuckin' kid gave me every reason from being able to grow a beard since he was five to the last reason he ever gave me. That reason was why I took him He was alone. That was it. He didn't tell me out of pity. He told me that so I would know that he was just like all of us. Before we foun each other, every one of us was alone in one way or another. Mouse didn't want to be a tough guy. Mouse saw our family, and he wanted to be a part of it."

I bite my lip, fighting back the fresh wave of sadness that washes over me and watch as Gunner places his hand on Mouse's casket

"The day I told that kid he was our newest prospect, the crazy bastard hooted and hollered like a fuckin' lunatic. Almost broke my goddamned ribs when he hugged me. I thought for sure this kid would fail. There's no way a kid like him would make it in a world like ours. But I was wrong — Mouse was the most faithful, lovin' kid I ever met. No matter what task I gave him, or how much I rode his ass, he did his job, and at the end of the day showed back up at the clubhouse with a smile on his fuckin' face. There was no breakin' Mouse."

"Like Mouse, there is no breakin' the Kings of Korruption either. His death is gonna be hard on all of us, but it won't go unpunished. Mouse will be avenged, if it's the last fuckin' thing I do." He looks to Sarah and places his hand over his chest. "Sarah, know that Mouse loved you and the very idea of that baby you're carrying made him the happiest man in the world. Know that Mouse was family to us, and that makes you and your little girl family too. We will always be here for both of you. Mouse wouldn't have it any other way."

Sarah sobs and clutches Tess tighter as she nods at Gunner, clearly thankful for his words. I look down at Laynie, finding her clutching onto Charlie with one arm as she holds tightly to my side. Sniffing, she wipes at her tear streaked face with a soggy tissue and smiles in my direction.

"You OK?"

"I'm OK, babe," I whisper.

She rests her head on my shoulder and sighs. "Good. Now lead me to the whiskey."

Shaking my head, I chuckle. Crazy.

Tease

GUNNER HAD LAID out the plan for us before we'd hit the road
for the five-hour trek to Toronto. We will go to the Devil's Rejects
clubhouse, take out whatever sorry excuse for a prospect they got
standing sentry at the gate and walk right in, shooting every fucker
we see along the way. Our main target is the President of the Devils
himself, Deed Landry. When all that's done, we torch the fucking
place.

After a long history with Deed and his Devils, we had finally
been starting to develop a friendship between the two clubs. Running
Laynie and me off the road had severed that friendship, and killing
Mouse had been the final nail in that motherfucker's coffin. He
doesn't stand a chance.

This whole plan is crazy – straight out of a fucking gangster
movie – but it's crazy enough that it just might work. The Devils
aren't going to be expecting us to walk in, bullets flying. They won't
be ready, and that gives us the element of surprise. The Devil's
clubhouse is an old warehouse on the outskirts of Toronto, far from
the busy residential and high traffic streets. They're going to hear us
coming, so we have to move fast.

Pulling to a stop several blocks from our target, Gunner turns to address us all. A fluttery feeling takes over my chest, and every muscle in my body tightens as he nails each of us to the spot with his eyes. "I hate this shit as much as you do. The truth is, I don't take killin' people lightly. But these fuckers killed Mouse. The next time, it could be any one of you."

His eyes dart to Ryker. "Or Charlie." He looks to me. "Or Laynie." My jaw clenches. It almost fucking was.

"Wait!" As one, we all turn to Ryker in surprise. "Are we really just gonna go in there, like a bunch of cold-blooded killers and kill these stupid fucks?"

Gunner steps forward and glares at Ryker. "The plan is set."

Ryker nods. "I know, but hear me out. If we follow through with this plan, we're no fuckin' better than they are." He flings his arms out and looks around. "Can all of you really live, knowing we just walked in and killed a bunch of men? Do you really think the fuckin' cops aren't goin' to track this back to us? That we aren't going to get caught?" He spears his hand through his hair. "One man ordered that drive-by. One man is behind those bastards comin' in and killin' Mouse. Let's play this shit smart and get rid of that one man."

Gunner's glare fades as he listens. "What are you suggestin'?"

"I say we wait. We watch that fuckin' clubhouse and wait for Deed to leave. Then we follow him home. After that, we get ahold of him and make that fucker pay."

I look around and watch as the other guys nod, and it's as if a giant weight is lifted from my chest. I wasn't afraid to carry out Gunner's plan, but the idea of killing so many people, of having their blood on my hands and of getting caught and having to leave Laynie to spend the rest of my life in jail had been a heavy weight on my mind.

Gunner nods. "Let's put it to a vote." He looks around at each of us. "All in favor of carrying out Ryk's plan, say aye." The ayes are unanimous.

Reaper and Jase move closer to the clubhouse and watch for Deed to leave. They are going to follow him home and call us with the location once he's settled inside.

We wait another four hours before Ryker gets a text from Jase saying that they're on the move. It's another hour after that before we get an address. As one, we ride together to the address Jase had provided.

Deed lives in a beaten-down, old farm house, several miles from his nearest neighbor. Reaper and Jase have already broken in and have him tied up on the floor of his living room. Deed glares at us all as we walk in, silent behind the gag tied around his head. His eyes narrow on Ryker.

"Yeah, it's me, motherfucker," Ryker says as he steps forward, his voice dripping with contempt. "You're a fuckin' idiot, Deed." Deed can do nothing but shoot hatred from his eyes. "This shit all started because *your* fuckin' guy tried to rape my wife. Nearly fuckin' killed her. Turnin' him in was the only fuckin' option we had, 'cause my girl needed a fuckin' ambulance to save her goddamned life. You wanted him, and it fuckin' killed me not to be the one to kill that prick, but I made you a fuckin' promise." He stabs a finger in Deed's face. "We had nothin' to do with Krueger bein' killed. You started this whole war over somethin' we didn't even fuckin' do."

Crouching down, he puts his face in Deed's. "You almost killed my buddy over there, and his girlfriend, over something we didn't fuckin' do." Ryker's voice raises as he speaks, face reddening with his anger. "You shot up our fuckin' day at the goddamned beach over some stupid fuckin' shit that we *didn't fuckin' do.*" He grabs the front of Deed's shirt and yanks him up off the floor, putting his nose only inches from Deed's. "And you killed our fuckin' prospect over SOME FUCKIN' SHIT THAT WE DID NOT DO!" he roars.

Deed's face pales, but his expression never changes. Ryker snorts in disgust and drops him, Deed's head cracking off the hardwood floor as he lands. Gunner steps forward and grabs Ryker's arm. "What do you wanna do?"

Ryker's fist tighten and his jaw clenches. Turning, he addresses us all. "That cocksucker has fucked us all." He yanks a large buck knife from a holster on his ankle. Deed's eyes widen. "We each deserve a crack at him. I say we string the fucker up so we can look im right in the eye. Then, one by one, we tell this useless sack of hit what he took from us, and then we take our stab. When it's all done, we set this shit farmhouse on fire and go the hell home."

One by one, we all nod, ignoring the fear in Deed's eyes. Reaper and Jase grab Deed, and using the long end of the rope they'd used to tie him up, hang him from the wrists to the exposed beams in the ceiling. My heart pounds and the blood rushes behind my ears as Reaper takes the knife from Ryker and approaches Deed once more.

"That fuckin' kid you killed? He was gonna be a fuckin' father. You robbed a baby girl of her fuckin' Daddy, you sick fuck." Rearing his arm back, he uses all his strength to ram the knife forward into Deed's belly.

It takes every ounce of self-control I have in me not to flinch. I watch as Jase approaches, taking the bloody knife from Reaper and steps up to Deed, whose screams of pain are muffled behind his gag. 'That kid was one of the most optimistic people I knew. He never hurt anyone in his life, and you fuckin' took that from him. From us." Clenching his teeth, Jase drives the blade into Deed's side.

Fighting back the nausea, I watch as one by one, each of the brothers jam that blade into Deed's flesh and tell him what he's done. When my turn comes, I step forward and take the blade from Ryker. I don't know if I can do this. Deed is nearly unconscious as he hangs limply from the ceiling, blood streaming down his body. But then I think back to the motorcycle ride I'd been on with Laynie, when Deed's goons had run us off the road. I think of the fear she must have felt when I didn't answer her after that crash. And then I think about the day that Mouse had been shot. Of the way Laynie had screamed and pleaded for help, and how she looked with tears and blood splattered on her face.

Stepping up to him, I use my finger to lift his chin. "You almost had me killed. You almost killed my woman. You did kill my brother. You're a waste of fuckin' oxygen." Driving my knife into his belly yet again, I watch as the life slowly drains from his eyes.

Taking a step back, I turn to the others. Everyone is standing there, arms at their sides, shoulders heaving with the heaviness of their breaths. Gunner is the first to walk away. Looking to Reaper, he calls out, "Burn this shit hole to the ground."

As I step outside, I hear a muffled voice coming from around the side of the house. "If you're comin', you better fuckin' come now 'cause Deed ain't gonna last much longer. These bastards have sliced him all to hell."

My blood starts to boil as I look around the corner of the house. Tiny stands there with his back to me, one hand on his hip, the other holding a cell phone to his ear. That betraying son-of-a-bitch.

"I don't fuckin' know. I'll stall them for as long as I can, but you better fuckin' hurry."

He ends the call and turns to walk back to the house, almost running into me. Raising one eyebrow, I watch as his face pales. "Who were you talkin' to, Tiny?"

He stands up straighter. "None of your fuckin' business, scar face."

My fist crashes into his face, flattening his nose on contact. "I'm gonna ask one last fuckin' time. Who the fuck were you talkin' to?"

Ryker and Gunner come around the corner as Tiny rolls around on the ground, clutching his hands over his nose. "You crazy fuck. You broke my fuckin' nose!"

Turning to Gunner, I struggle to calm the fuck down and explain what I heard. "That fat fuck was talkin' to someone. Sounded like he was tellin' them where we are and what we were doin' to Deed."

Ryker's eyes bulge and his fists tighten as he takes a step forward, but Gunner raises his hand. "Give me the phone."

Tiny stops his bitching, fear filling his eyes as he watches me pick up the cell phone he'd used and hand it to Gunner. Gunner taps the screen a few times and puts the phone to his ear, his eyes never leaving Tiny's prone position on the ground. A muffled greeting comes from it and Gunner's eyes close. Disconnecting the call, he looks to Ryker. "Seems like Tiny here's been talkin' to the Devil's fuckin' VP."

Rage pins me in place as I stare at Tiny. Ryker's foot flies out kicking him in the ribs. "Fuck!"

"I didn't tell them shit!" Tiny gasps between desperate gasps for air.

Gunner hands the phone to Ryker. "Go through it. See how often he talks to these assholes. And for how long." Reaching down, he grabs Tiny by the collar and pulls him to his feet. I step forward and hold his arms behind his back as Gunner searches him, pulling three different guns from his holsters.

Ryker taps the screen, searching through the call history, his face darkening with every tap. His eyes flick to Tiny. "Explain."

"Fuck you," he spits, hatred shining brightly in his eyes.

Ryker holds up the phone, his jaw tight. "Says here you had a seven-minute conversation with Deed himself the night Tease and Laynie got ran off the road."

Tiny says nothing.

Ryker continues. "It also says here that you spoke to him again, for eleven minutes this time, the morning of our little picnic. The same day those fuckers swooped in and killed Mouse."

He tries to back up, but I hold his arms tightly. Gunner takes the phone from Ryker and turns to face Tiny. "So, these assholes are on their way here now?"

He glares at us all as he spits on the ground.

Gunner gives a curt nod and reaches behind him, pulling out his gun. Tiny's eyes widen a fraction, but he doesn't say anything. Gunner raises the gun, pointing it in Tiny's face. He looks to me, and flicks his eyes to the side, indicating that I need to step away. I drop Tiny's arms and move to stand behind Gunner.

Gunner narrows his eyes, hate etched heavily on his features. "Guess we don't have time to put it to a vote." Then he pulls the trigger.

Turning to me, he stuffs the gun back in his pocket. "Put him in the house so he can burn with his buddy Deed, and let's get the fuck home to our women."

Laynie

Sighing, I touch the screen, accepting the phone call from my mother. "Hi, Mom."

Her voice is quiet when she responds. "Hi, Laynie." Surprised by the uneasiness in her voice, I wait. "I'm glad you answered."

"You OK, Mom?" Worry creeps into my mind while I listen to her take a deep breath.

"I'm sorry, Laynie." Her words wash over me, shock freezing my tongue. "I've been doing some thinking since I talked to your young man …" She takes a deep breath. "He was right, you know? What he said. I knew he was right. I just couldn't accept it." Her voice fills with tears. "You and I used to be so close, honey. And I ruined that."

Tears fill my eyes as I listen to her confession. "No, Mom. You didn't ruin it." I smile. "You may have squashed it a bit, but you didn't ruin it."

She chokes out a laugh through her tears. "I'm going to work on being so overprotective, OK? I just…after the accident, I think I just started focusing on you to help concentrate on something other than losing Garrett. I almost lost you too, Laynie. There was a while there when we didn't know if you were going to make it. It was terrifying."

Tears slip down my cheeks. Sometimes I forget that even though I had lost my vision and my brother in the accident, my parents had lost a son. Hearing her admit to that pain makes me realize just how selfish my thinking has been.

"I love you, Mom."

She sobs into the phone. "Oh, baby, I love you too."

My mom and I stay on the phone for another twenty minutes, and when we finally hang up, my heart feels lighter than it has in years. Things are finally working out with my mother, and my dad and I have always been solid. He's wonderful, but he avoids confrontation at all costs. I know he loves me, but he never gets in my face. As for Daniel, I need to fix things with him still, but at least we're talking.

Hearing the key in the lock, I sit up, waiting for Travis to get inside. Though he wouldn't tell me where he was going, I knew. It was in the heaviness of his voice, and the whispered telephone calls, not to mention the fact that he has been gone so long.

"Hi." He sounds exhausted.

I smile and hold my arms out, motioning for him to come to me.

"Hi, honey."

The couch dips as he settles down beside me, dragging me up onto his lap and wrapping his arms around me tightly. Pressing his lips to the top of my head, he just holds me. He smells like soap and laundry detergent.

"You were gone a while," I whisper.

He nods, lips still pressed to my hair. "I got back a couple hours ago. Stopped by my place to have a shower first."

I say nothing and just squeeze him tight.

"Fuck. I'm so glad to be home, Laynie."

My heart squeezes and my belly flutters. Squeezing him even tighter, I whisper, "I'm glad too, honey."

We sit in silence, holding each other, and just listening to our breathing. Finally, I can't stand it anymore. "Are you OK, Travis?"

He shakes his head, his lips twisting in my hair as he does. "No."

I turn, placing my hands on his cheeks and press my lips to his. "Tell me."

He shakes his head again. "I can't. If you don't know anything, you can't get into any trouble."

Swallowing, I nod. I knew it was bad. "I know you went after the Devils."

He freezes. "How the fuck do you know that?"

"Just the way you've been acting. The whispered phone calls the last couple of days, and the fact that you were gone so long." I sweep my lips across his cheek. "You don't have to tell me anything, but you can talk to me."

Sighing, he picks me up and sets me back on the couch before he stands. I can hear him pacing back and forth in front of me as he talks. "Fuck. That shit we did…while I was away…it was fuckin' bad, Laynie. How can we live with ourselves after that shit?"

Forcing my face to remain expressionless, I keep it pointed straight ahead as I answer him. "Is it over?"

He snorts. "Oh, it's over." He goes back to pacing. "Do you believe in an eye for an eye, Laynie? Retribution?"

Biting my lip, I think about his question. I think about Mouse, and Sarah, and the baby that she's carrying. Then I think about how those men had pulled up to that picnic area, opened fire on us and drove away without the cops being able to do a damn thing about it. Clenching my fists, I set my jaw and nod. "Absolutely."

Air rushes from his lungs and he kneels in front of me, placing his hands on my knees. "Just when I was starting to believe I wasn' a monster…"

Running my fingers through his hair, I aim my eyes at his face and whisper, "Monsters don't feel remorse. Monsters are people like those men, who come along and steal a precious life, then move on like nothing happened. You're not a monster, Travis. You're human."

His fingertips trail across my cheeks. "You make me want to believe that."

I smile softly. "You should. It's true."

He sighs. "Laynie, my world is fucked-up. I'm not some fairytale biker from one of your books, and I don't live in a fairytale biker world. It's real and it's fuckin' dangerous."

Smirking, I nod. "Getting run off the road clued me in on that. Getting shot at confirmed it."

"Jesus," he mutters.

Biting back a smile, I sigh. "I know it's not like my books, Travis. I know that it's dangerous. But do you wanna know something? I don't care. Since I met you, my life has gone from lonely and dark to exciting and full of color. I've made new friends and had more adventures than any of the heroines in my books." I smile. "Best of all, I have you. You are the first man to ever look past my blindness and treat me like a normal human being. The first man to ever make me *feel* like I'm special." Nuzzling my face into his hand, I continue, "Who cares if it's dangerous? I'm not afraid of living this life with you. I'm more afraid of living it without you."

He's silent a moment before laying his head on my lap. "Fuck, I love you," he whispers.

"I love you too, honey."

Epilogue

Laynie

IT'S BEEN THREE months since that terrible day that Mouse was ripped away from us all. Since then, not a night has gone by that Travis hasn't slept in my bed. No matter what either of us had going on that day, at the end of the night, we crawled into bed together, falling asleep in one another's arms, and waking up every morning in a tangle of arms and legs and tousled hair.

Today we'd made it official. Travis had packed up the few things that he owned and moved them into my apartment. Already I had tripped over his enormous motorcycle boots, almost fallen in the toilet after he'd left the seat up, and had put my hand in a small puddle of mysterious liquid that he'd left on the counter. It seems living together for real is going to take some getting used to.

Hearing the water turn off in the shower, I fluff up my hair one last time and make sure to position myself in what I can only hope is a sexy position. As soon as Travis had gotten into the shower, I'd run to the closet and pulled out my favorite high-heeled shoes and stripped off my clothes, leaving only my lacy thong panties. I'd then found his leather cut and pulled it on as well. Now, I'm standing in the doorway to the bedroom, hand propped on one hip while I wait for my man to get out of the shower.

I hear him enter and hear the whisper of a towel running across his wet skin, then his deep intake of breath.

"Jesus," he whispers.

Smiling, I place my finger inside the opening to the cut I'm wearing and slowly trail it down between my breasts and down my belly, slipping it just inside the band of my panties.

"Stop," he orders in a deep, husky voice. I pause, pulling my lower lip between my teeth. I hear his footsteps as he approaches me. "Don't fuckin' move."

The sound of his knees hitting the floor in front of me takes my breath away. My smile fades as my heart races. Uncertainty starts to creep in as I wait for him to do something, say something…to touch me.

His breaths come out in jagged pants. "Fuck, Laynie. You fuckin' wreck me." My belly flutters at the sound of his strangled voice. "You are the most beautiful fuckin' woman I've ever seen." His fingertips slip inside the cut and trail slowly up my belly. "You have no fuckin' clue how incredible you are," he whispers.

Parting the cut slowly, his other hand slips inside. He cups my breasts with both hands, rolling my nipples between his finger and thumb. Heat builds low in my belly. I can feel the wetness between my legs soaking into my panties.

I can feel his warm breath on my mound through the lace of my panties just before I feel the firm swipe of his tongue through my folds. Pleasure spikes through me, almost bringing me to my knees. His tongue pushes against my panties once more and drags slowly across my clit.

I reach down and spear his hair with my fingers as he laps at my swollen bud and continues to roll my nipples with his magic fingers. I whimper in protest when he pulls away, only to cry out in shock when his hands go between my legs, tearing the thin strip of fabric that covers my wet entrance, leaving it hanging uselessly from my waist.

"Those were my sexiest panties!"

"I'll buy you more," he growls, and then his mouth is on me. Lifting my leg, he places it over his shoulder as his mouth sucks at

144

ny heated clit. I throw my head back and grab onto the door frame with both hands to steady myself.

Continuing to fuck me with his mouth, he reaches up and pinches my nipple once more, causing the most beautiful pain I've ever known. I rock my hips against his stubbled face, my orgasm building strong and fast. When his finger plunges deep inside of me, I scream out as the pleasure overwhelms me, my entire body trembling with my release.

When my cries stop and my body relaxes, Travis stands and takes my mouth in a hard, hungry kiss. Molding my body to his, I allow his kiss to sweep me away to a place where there is only him and me – forever. Love for him swells in my heart as my tongue tangles with his.

He pulls away and whisks what's left of my panties down my legs. As I lift my foot to remove my shoes, he grabs my wrist and growls. "Keep 'em on."

Arching an eyebrow, I smirk and follow him to the bed where he's leading me by the hand. "Yes, sir."

Positioning my body where he wants it, he places his hand between my shoulder blades and pushes my upper body down on the bed, my ass up high in the air. Moaning, he trails his finger down my back and over my ass until he sweeps it through my wetness to circle my sensitive clit. I scream out, heat building once more as he gives it a tight pinch. "This isn't the time for you to be a smartass, Laynie."

Panting, I roll my hips, desperate for him to touch me again. "It's all I know how to be."

My breath catches in my throat and my skin stings in my new favorite way as his hand comes down with a sharp slap on the globe of my ass. "Let's see if we can't teach you to be a little nicer."

"I ain't nice," I whisper, echoing his words from long ago.

I hear a soft chuckle and then another slap lands, causing my pussy to clench tight in anticipation. "No. You're not. You're a smartass." His fingers find my clit once more, and I close my eyes, moaning as he circles them around it, bringing another orgasm close to the surface.

Just as I'm about to cum, he pulls them away. Whimpering, I lift my head to turn and beg him when he enters me from behind, driving himself all the way to the hilt. Our mutual groans of pleasurecho through the room.

Travis continues to drive into me, our heavy breaths and thsound of our skin slapping together the only sounds I can hear. Hfeels so good inside of me. So right. As his hand comes down on monce more, my pussy clamps around him, holding him in place.

"Jesus, babe," he says through gritted teeth. "Seein' my pinhandprint on your ass drives me fuckin' crazy."

Reaching down and back between us, I gently cup his balls anroll them in my hand, earning me a sharp gasp. "Shut up and fucme, Travis."

He doesn't even bother with a reply. Flipping me to my back, hsettles himself between my legs and claims my mouth at the samtime that he pushes himself inside of me. Rolling my hips along witlhis, I cry out once more as my release takes over my body. Feelinhis cock swell and hearing his groan, I squeeze my pussy tight aTravis cums with me.

When the pleasure fades and our bodies stop trembling, our kisses slow from frantic to sweet. Travis pulls away and pushes my haiback from my sweaty brow. "Love you, babe."

Smiling brightly, I whisper back, "Love you too." Resting myhead on his shoulder, I give him a squeeze and close my eyes. Just asleep begins to take over, his quiet voice brings me back to the present.

"My life is so different with you." He places a kiss on top of myhead. "It's almost perfect."

"Almost?"

He nods against the top of my head. "Can you come somewherwith me?"

"Anywhere."

Tease

Pulling up to the cemetery, I park my bike along the narrow road an

wing my leg off. Reaching out, I grasp Laynie's hand and help her
o the ground. I watch as she shakes out her hair after taking off the
helmet, a lump forming in my throat. My mind races for any excuse
o not do this. I don't *want* to fucking do this, but Laynie's right: if I
ever have any chance to live a happy life, I need to get rid of the poison in my soul.

She reaches out and places a hand on my cheek. "Hey. You can
do this, honey. Tell her what you need to say."

I look away, unable to deal with the love shining in her sightless
eyes. "This is fuckin' useless. The bitch is dead."

She presses on my cheek, turning me to face her again. "It's not.
She's dead, Travis, but you're not. You're the one left living with
the hate and the anger." She smiles a sad smile. "Forgiveness is a
choice. It's a choice you don't have to make if you don't want to, but
I will tell you right now…forgiveness really is divine. It will give
you the power to finally let go of all that hurt, and bitterness, and
anger that has been eating away at you for years. Forgiveness is a
way of taking back that power, so you can move on and finally live
your life with true peace."

I can't take my eyes off of her while she speaks, the love I feel
for her making my heart swell. "How'd you get so smart?"

She grins. "Oh, I'm the total package, baby. Grace, brains and
beauty." She winks. "I'm really bendy too."

Wrapping my arms around her, I burst out laughing. This woman
is everything to me. I know I'll never have the words to properly tell
her just what she's done for me, and how much she means to me, but
I want to spend every moment making her feel it. Hugging her close,
I brush my lips against her temple and whisper, "Love you, babe."

"I love you too, Travis," she whispers back.

Pulling back slowly, I take her hand and move to toward the area
I was told my mother was buried. After doing a little digging, Reaper had managed to find out what had become of my mother and
Rick. My mother had died less than a year after I had run away. She
was found in a tub full of bloody water, with her wrists slit and
bruises all over body. Her arm was broken and there was a large
gash on the side of her head.

Rick was sentenced to life in prison for her murder. He'd tried to make it look like a suicide but the obvious injuries on her body left no question as to what had really fucking happened. He spent six years in jail before another inmate shanked him with a homemade shiv. I wish he was still alive so I could shank the fucker myself.

I am scanning the numbers on every plot when her name catches my eye. "Deborah Hale." My heart constricts when I see that who ever had arranged her burial had buried her with my father's name and not Rick's. That's the way it should be.

I stop and let go of Laynie's hand. She stands back and waits quietly while I trace my fingers lightly over the letters of her name. think back to the memories I have from before my dad died. My mother had been so beautiful and fun. I remember her singing in the kitchen as she baked us chocolate chip cookies and dancing around the living room when her favorite song came on the radio. I remember her wiping my forehead with a cool cloth when I had a fever and crawling into bed with me when I had a nightmare.

After my dad had died, she changed. I remember the distant look on her face when Rick hit me, and the smell of stale alcohol that seemed to follow her everywhere she went. I remember the nights I spent with belly cramps because they went to bed without making supper and the many days I had to wear dirty clothes because my mom had forgotten to do laundry. But then I think about the other memories. The fights she used to have with Rick, and the screams I'd hear as she pleaded with him to stop hitting her. I remember the black eyes and the look of defeat she wore every day when she finally crawled out of bed.

And then I think back to that day in the police station. She wouldn't even look at me that day. Crouched low in front of my mother's headstone, I place my hand on top and squeeze my eyes closed. My mother had finally done something to save me that day. She had no way of knowing the shit I would go through in foster care. She let me go because she knew I wasn't safe in her house.

A tear slips from my eye and rolls slowly down my cheek as I remember the tears I'd seen her cry in that police interrogation room. She'd been setting me free. My mother had been just as afraid and ust as trapped in that house as I was, but she had finally been able to help set me free.

Understanding flows through me, the love I had for my mother burning brighter than it had in over twenty years. Turning, I take the small bouquet of flowers that Laynie's holding and prop them up gently against her stone. I reach up and run my fingers across her name once more and whisper through the gravel in my voice, "Thank you."

I stare at her name for another moment, thinking about all those years I'd wasted, hating my mother before I finally stand and turn toward Laynie. Stepping into her, I kiss her forehead and hold her close. "And thank *you*," I whisper.

Popping up on the tips of her toes, she places a gentle kiss on my cheek. "How do you feel?"

Wrapping my arms around her, I pull her up off her feet and whisper into her ear. "Free."

Jase

I watch her ass sway and bounce to the beat of the music, my dick hardening and pressing tightly against the zipper of my jeans. I can't take my fucking eyes off her. I'd noticed Ellen months ago, when she was one of the nurses at the hospital where my buddy Smokey had gone to die. She was fucking gorgeous in scrubs, but seeing her long legs and tight ass in that little black skirt makes my heart skip a beat.

"Don't even think about it, man."

I look at Reaper and smirk. "Think about what?"

He snorts, shaking his head. "Charlie fuckin' asked you to stay away from that bitch. It's one woman. Pick a different one."

I cast my eyes back to the dancefloor and watch as Ellen swivels her hips and laughs along with her friends. Charlie had told me to stay away from her more than once, and so far I'd listened, but watching her dance, head thrown back with laughter, I'm not sure I can do that anymore. For months I've had glimpses of her, and every time, I flirted and she laughed, but for the most part, I've kept my distance. Not anymore. *Sorry, Charlie.*

"Come on, Reap. Look at those other bitches. Be a decent fuckin wingman, would ya."

He raises his brows. "I'm not anyone's wingman. I can find bitches all on my own."

I shrug and throw my hands up. "Your loss, brother."

Leaving Reaper on his own, I weave my way through the throng of dancing bodies and approach the group of ladies to come up behind Ellen. The women in her circle exchange glances of surprise but nobody says a word as I slip my hands onto her narrow waist and dance along behind her.

The minute my hands touch her body, she spins around, pinning me with an annoyed glare. Once she realizes who it is, the glare fades and uncertainty takes over. Raising my eyebrows, I give her my sexiest smile. It never fails.

Smirking slightly, she shakes her head and leans forward, shouting over the music. "What are you doing?"

I grab onto her hips once again, and drag her into me, pressing her body against mine. Using the loud music as an excuse to lean into her, I shout back. "Well I *was* dancing with you."

Pulling back, she places her hands on my chest and pushes me away gently. "I don't think that's a good idea, Jase."

What the fuck? "Why not?"

Biting the inside of her lip, she looks into my eyes and shakes her head once more. "It just isn't."

My gut sinks as she turns and walks off the dance floor without looking back. I'm in shock. This has never fucking happened before. Not to me, anyways. I look over at the three ladies that Ellen had been dancing with. All three of them are still dancing but have their eyes on me. One of them shakes her head, giving me a slight shrug.

Frowning, I turn and watch as Ellen gets closer to the washrooms. *That's it? It just isn't? I don't think so.* Avoiding the swaying bodies, spilling drinks, and the grabby hands of one very drunk woman, I wind my way through the crowd once more and lean against the wall outside the ladies room. I wait for almost five minutes before Ellen comes back out.

It's quieter back here so I don't have to shout. "How do you know?"

She yelps in surprise and freezes, wide eyes on mine. "What?"

I take a step forward. "How do you know that it's not a good idea?"

She stares at me a moment, like a deer caught in the headlights. Then she recovers. Rolling her eyes, she chuckles. "It was just a dance, Jase."

I take another step forward, closing in on her space in the narrow hallway. "Exactly. It was just a dance. How can that be a bad idea?"

Pressing her back against the wall, her chuckle falling away as she nibbles on her lip, her eyes never leaving mine. "Jase …" Her shoulders slump, and she lets out a heavy sigh. "Look…you're a nice guy, but …"

Placing my hand on the wall above her head, I lean forward and recapture her eyes with mine. "It was just a dance, Elle."

Standing up straighter, she gives me a challenging look. "Really."

Chuckling, I nod my head but whisper, "Fuck no."

Her eyes widen, and she pushes off the wall, making me take a step back. "That's why. I'm not that girl, Jase. I don't do one-night stands. I've heard all about you, Jase Matthews"

"Ah, so you've been asking around about me."

She narrows her eyes and shakes her head. "No. But I've heard enough to know a few things, and more than enough to know that I am most certainly not what you're looking for."

The smile falls from my face as annoyance seeps in. "And what exactly do you think I'm looking for?"

She shakes her head. "Not me." On that final note, she turns and walks away.

I watch in confusion as she fades back into the crowd. *What the fuck just happened?* I've never been blown off like that before. *Women love me. I'm Jase Motherfucking Matthews.*

I emerge from the hallway just as Ellen and her friends are walking out of the bar. Just before she walks out, she turns and our eyes lock. Even from the other side of the room, I can see her hesitation before she turns and leaves. *Oh yeah...she's exactly what I'm look ing for. She just doesn't know it yet.*

Jase

Book Three in the Kings of Korruption MC series
Out now!

About Geri

Geri Glenn lives in beautiful New Brunswick, Canada. She is an army wife, the mother of two gorgeous but slightly crazy little girls, and just recently is fortunate enough to quit her day job to stay home and do what she loves most - write!

Geri has been as avid reader for as long as she can remember. When she isn't writing or adulting in some other fashion, she can usually be found curled up in a comfy chair, reading on her iPad both day and night. Geri is an incurable night owl, and it's not uncommon for her to still be awake reading at 4 am, just because she finds it hard to put the book down.

Geri loves all genres of fiction, but her passion is anything romantic or terrifying; basically, anything that can get her heart pumping. This passion has bled out onto her laptop and become the Kings of Korruption.

Writing that first book in the series has knocked off the #1 thing on Geri's bucket list, and publishing it has been an absolute dream come true. She hopes you love the Kings as much as she does.

Stalk her!

♛ Facebook: https://www.facebook.com/geriglennauthor

♛ Twitter: https://twitter.com/authorgeriglenn

♛ Instagram: https://instagram.com/authorgeriglenn/

♛ Website: http://geriglenn.com/

Made in the USA
Lexington, KY
04 July 2018